DAYMARE

AND OTHER TALES FROM THE PULPS

DAYMARE

AND OTHER TALES FROM THE PULPS

FREDRIC BROWN

WILDSIDE PRESS

DAYMARE AND OTHER TALES FROM THE PULPS

"Daymare" originally appeared in
Thrilling Wonder Stories, Fall 1943. "The Little Lamb" originally
appeared in *Manhunt,* August 1953. "The Geezenstacks"
originally appeared in *Weird Tales,* September 1943. "The Hat
Trick" (published under the pseudonym "Felix Graham")
originally appeared in *Unknown,* February 1942.
"Arena" originally appeared in *Astounding,* June 1942. "Don't
Look Behind You," originally appeared in *Ellery Queen's Mystery
Magazine,* May 1947.

CONTENTS

INTRODUCTION 7

DAYMARE 9

THE LITTLE LAMB 55

THE GEEZENSTACKS 68

THE HAT TRICK 79

ARENA 86

DON'T LOOK BEHIND YOU 114

INTRODUCTION

Fredric Brown (1906–1972) was a writer of mysteries and science fiction — sometimes both at the same time, as with the title story of this collection, "Daymare." He was a newspaperman for most of his adult life, and only spent 14 years as a full-time writer. He was married twice and had two sons. His work reflects his varied interests, including chess, poker, and the works of Lewis Carroll.

His first published mystery was "The Moon for a Nickel" in 1939; his first published work of science fiction was "Not Yet the End," which appeared in *Captain Future* magazine in 1941. Over the next twenty-six years, he produced a steady stream of stories for the pulps of the day. You could sometimes find three or four of his works in different magazines on the newsstand at the same time.

Nor did he neglect longer forms. Brown published a number of great novels, including *What Mad Universe* (1949), *The Lights in the Sky Are Stars* (1953), and *Martians, Go Home* (1955) in the science fiction genre; and *The Fabulous Clipjoint* (1946), *The Screaming Mimi* (1949), and *The Far Cry* (1951) in the mystery genre. *The Fabulous Clipjoint* won an Edgar Award from the Mystery Writers of America for Best First Novel.

Even so, Fredric Brown remains best-known for his short fiction. His short story "Arena" (in this volume) became the basis for a *Star Trek* episode of the same title. The original story was voted by the membership of the Science Fiction Writers of America as one of the twenty finest SF stories of all time. Many of Brown's short-short stories are also classics of the field.

This volume is an excellent starting place for readers new to Fredric Brown's work, since it samples his stories in several different genres. Long-time fans looking for rare and favorite tales will not be disappointed, either. Enjoy!

— *John Gregory Betancourt*

DAYMARE

CHAPTER ONE

Five Way Corpse

IT started out like a simple case of murder. That was bad enough in itself, because it was the first murder during the five years Rod Caquer had been Lieutenant of Police in Sector Three of Callisto. Sector Three was proud of that record, or had been until the record became a dead duck. But before the thing was over, nobody would have been happier than Rod Caquer if it had stayed a simple case of murder — without cosmic repercussions.

Events began to happen when Rod Caquer's buzzer made him look up at the visiscreen. There he saw the image of Barr Maxon, Regent of Sector Three.

"Morning, Regent," Caquer said pleasantly. "Nice speech you made last night on the —"

Maxon cut him short. "Thanks, Caquer," he said. "You know Willem Deem?"

"The book-and-reel shop proprietor? Yes, slightly."

"He's dead," announced Maxon. "It seems to be murder. You better go there."

His image clicked off the screen before Caquer could ask any questions. But the questions could wait anyway. He was already on his feet and buckling on his short-sword.

Murder on Callisto? It did not seem possible, but if it had really happened he should get there quickly. Very quickly, if he was to have time for a look at the body before they took it to the incinerator.

On Callisto, bodies are never held for more than an hour after death because of the hylra spores which, in minute quantity, are always present in the thinnish atmosphere. They are harmless, of course, to live tissue, but they tremendously accelerate the rate of putrefaction in dead animal matter of any sort.

Dr. Skidder, the Medico-in-Chief, was coming out the front door of the book-and-reel shop when Lieutenant Caquer arrived there, breathless. The medico jerked a thumb back over his shoulder.

"Better hurry if you want a look," he said to Caquer. "They're taking it out the back way. But I've examined —"

Caquer ran on past him and caught the white-uniformed utility men at the back door of the shop.

"Hi, boys, let me take a look," Caquer cried as he peeled back the sheet that covered the thing on the stretcher.

It made him feel a bit sickish, but there was not any doubt of the identity of the corpse or the cause of death. He had hoped against hope that it would turn out to have been an accidental death after all. But the skull had been cleaved down to the eyebrows — a blow struck by a strong man with a heavy sword.

"Better let us hurry, Lieutenant. It's almost an hour since they found him."

Caquer's nose confirmed it, and he put the sheet back quickly and let the utility men go on to their gleaming white truck parked just outside the door.

He walked back into the shop thoughtfully and looked around. Everything seemed in order. The long shelves of cellu-wrapped merchandise were neat and orderly. The row of booths along the other side, some equipped with an enlarger for book customers and the others with projectors for those who were interested in the microfilms, were all empty and undisturbed.

A little crowd of curious persons was gathered outside the door; but Brager, one of the policemen, was keeping them out of the shop.

"Hey. Brager," said Caquer, and the patrolman came in and closed the door behind him.

"Yes, Lieutenant?"

"Know anything about this? Who found him, and when, and so on?"

"I did, almost an hour ago. I was walking by on my beat when I heard the shot."

Caquer looked at him blankly.

"The shot?" he repeated.

"Yeah. I ran in, and there he was dead and nobody around. I knew nobody had come out the front way, so I ran to the rear and there wasn't anybody in sight from the rear door. So I came back and put in the call."

"To whom? Why didn't you call me direct, Brager?"

"Sorry, Lieutenant, but I was excited and I pushed the wrong button and got the Regent. I told him somebody had shot Deem and he said stay on guard and he'd call the medico and the utility boys and you."

In that order? Caquer wondered. Apparently, because Caquer had been the last one to get there.

But he brushed that aside for the more important question — the matter of Brager having heard a shot. That did not make sense, unless . . . no, that was absurd, too. If Willem Deem had been shot, the medico would not have split his skull as part of the autopsy.

"What do you mean by a shot, Brager?" Caquer asked. "An old-fashioned explosive weapon?"

"Yeah," said Brager. "Didn't you see the body? A hole right over the heart. A bullet-hole, I guess. I never saw one before. I didn't know there was a gun on Callisto. They were outlawed even before the blasters were."

Caquer nodded slowly.

"You — you didn't see evidence of any other — uh — wound?" he persisted.

"Earth, no. Why would there be any other wound? A hole through a man's heart's enough to kill him, isn't it?"

"Where did Dr. Skidder go when he left here?" Caquer inquired. "Did he say?"

"Yeah, he said you would be wanting his report, so he'd

go back to his office and wait till you came around or called him. What do you want me to do, Lieutenant?"

Caquer thought a moment.

"Go next door and use the visiphone there, Brager — I'll be busy on this one," Caquer at last told the policeman. "Get three more men, and the four of you canvass this block and question everyone."

"You mean whether they saw anybody run out the back way, and if they heard the shot, and that sort of thing?" asked Brager.

"Yes. Also anything they may know about Deem, or who might have had a reason to — to shoot him."

Brager saluted, and left.

Caquer got Dr. Skidder on the visiphone.

"Hello, Doctor," he said. "Let's have it."

"Nothing but what met the eye, Rod. Blaster, of course. Close range."

Lieutenant Rod Caquer steadied himself. "Say that again, Medico."

"What's the matter," jibed Skidder. "Never see a blaster death before? Guess you wouldn't have at that, Rod, you're too young. But fifty years ago, when I was a student, we got them once in a while."

"Just how did it kill him?"

Dr. Skidder looked surprised. "Oh, you didn't catch up with the clearance men, then. I thought you'd seen it. Left shoulder, burned all the skin and flesh off and charred the bone. Actual death was from shock — the blast didn't hit a vital area. Not that the burn wouldn't have been fatal anyway, in all probability. But the shock made it instantaneous."

Dreams are like this, Caquer told himself. *In dreams things happen without meaning anything* he thought. *But I'm not dreaming, this is real.*

"Any other wounds, or marks on the body?" he asked, slowly.

"None. I'd suggest, Rod, you concentrate on a search for

that blaster. Search all of Sector Three, if you have to. You know what a blaster looks like, don't you?"

"I've seen pictures," said Caquer. "Do they make a noise, Medico? I've never seen one fired."

Dr. Skidder shook his head. "There's a flash and a hissing sound, but no report."

"It couldn't be mistaken for a gunshot?"

The doctor stared at him.

"You mean an explosive gun? Of course not. Just a faint *s-s-s-s*. One couldn't hear it more than ten feet away."

Lieutenant Caquer clicked off the visiphone, sat down, and closed his eyes to concentrate. Somehow, he had to make sense out of three conflicting sets of observations. His own, the patrolman's, and the medico's.

Brager had been the first one to see the body, and he said there was a hole over the heart. And that there were no other wounds. He had heard the report of the shot.

Caquer thought, *Suppose Brager is lying. It still doesn't make sense.* Because according to Dr. Skidder, there was no bullet-hole, but a blaster-wound. Skidder had seen the body after Brager had.

Someone could, theoretically at least, have used a blaster in the interim, on a man already dead. But . . .

But that did not explain the head wound, nor the fact that the medico had not seen the bullet hole.

Someone could, theoretically at least, have struck the skull with a sword between the time Skidder had made the autopsy and the time he, Rod Caquer, had seen the body. But . . .

But that didn't explain why he hadn't seen the charred shoulder when he'd lifted the sheet from the body on the stretcher. He might have missed seeing a bullet-hole; but he would not, and he could not, have missed seeing a shoulder in the condition Dr. Skidder described it.

Around and around it went, until at last it dawned on him that there was only one explanation possible. The Medico-in-Chief was lying, for whatever mad reason.

Brager's story could be true, in total. That meant, of course, that he, Rod Caquer, had overlooked the bullet hole Brager had seen; but that was possible.

But Skidder's story could not be true. Skidder himself, at the time of the autopsy, could have inflicted the wound in the head. And he could have lied about the shoulder-wound. Why — unless the man was mad — he would have done either of those things, Caquer could not imagine. But it was the only way he could reconcile all the factors.

But by now the body had been disposed of. It would be his word against Dr. Skidder's.

But wait! — the utility men, two of them, would have seen the corpse when they put it on the stretcher.

Quickly Caquer stood up in front of the visiphone and obtained a connection with utility headquarters.

"The two clearance men who took a body from Shop 9364 less than an hour ago — have they reported back yet?" he asked.

"Just a minute, Lieutenant . . . Yes, one of them was through for the day and went on home. The other one is here."

"Put him on."

Rod Caquer recognized the man who stepped into the screen. It was the one of the two utility men who had asked him to hurry.

"Yes, Lieutenant?" said the man.

"You helped put the body on the stretcher?"

"Of course."

"What would you say was the cause of death?"

The man in white looked out of the screen incredulously.

"Are you kidding me, Lieutenant?" he grinned. "Even a moron could see what was wrong with that stiff."

Caquer frowned.

"Nevertheless, there are conflicting statements. I want your opinion."

"Opinion? When a man has his head cut off, what two opinions can there be, Lieutenant?"

Caquer forced himself to speak calmly. "Will the man who went with you confirm that?"

"Of course. Earth's Oceans! We had to put it on the stretcher in two pieces. Both of us for the body, and then Walter picked up the head and put it on next to the trunk. The killing was done with a disintegrator beam, wasn't it?"

"You talked it over with the other man?" said Caquer. "There was no difference of opinion between you about the — uh — details?"

"Matter of fact there was. That was why I asked you if it was a disintegrator. After we'd cremated it, he tried to tell me the cut was a ragged one like somebody'd taken several blows with an axe or something. But it was clean."

"Did you notice evidence of a blow struck at the top of the skull?"

"No. Say, lieutenant, you aren't looking so well. Is anything the matter with you?"

CHAPTER II

Terror by Night

That was the setup that confronted Rod Caquer, and one cannot blame him for beginning to wish it had been a simple case of murder.

A few hours ago, it had seemed bad enough to have Callisto's no-murder record broken. But from there, it got worse. He did not know it then, but it was going to get still worse and that would be only the start.

It was eight in the evening, now, and Caquer was still at his office with a copy of Form 812 in front of him on the duraplast surface of his desk. There were questions on that form, apparently simple questions.

NAME OF DECEASED: *Willem Deem*
OCCUPATION: *Prop. of book-and-reel shop*

RESIDENCE: *Apt. 8250, Sector Three, Clsto.*
PLACE OF BUSINESS: *Shop 9364, S. T., Clsto.*
TIME OF DEATH: *Approx. 3 P.M. Clsto. Std. Time*
CAUSE OF DEATH:

Yes, the first five questions had been a breeze. But the six? He had been staring at that question an hour now. A Callisto hour, not so long as an Earth one, but long enough when you're staring at a question like that. Confound it, he would have to put something down.

Instead, he reached for the visiphone button, and a moment later Jane Gordon was looking at him out of the screen. And Rod Caquer looked back, because she was something to look at.

"Hello, Icicle," he said. "Afraid I'm not going to be able to get there this evening. Forgive me?"

"Of course, Rod. What's wrong? The Deem business?"

He nodded gloomily. "Desk work. Lot of forms and reports I got to get out for the Sector Coordinator."

"Oh. How was he killed, Rod?"

"Rule Sixty-five," he said with a smile, "forbids giving details of any unsolved crime to a civilian."

"Bother Rule Sixty-five. Dad knew Willem Deem well, and he's been a guest here often. Mr. Deem was practically a friend of ours."

"Practically?" Caquer asked. "Then I take it you didn't like him, Icicle?"

"Well — I guess I didn't. He was interesting to listen to, but he was a sarcastic little beast, Rod. I think he had a perverted sense of humor. How was he killed?"

"If I tell you, will you promise not to ask any more questions?" Caquer said with a sigh.

Her eyes lighted eagerly. "Of course."

"He was shot," said Caquer, "with an explosive-type gun and a blaster. Someone split his skull with a sword, chopped off his head with an axe and with a disintegrator beam. Then after he was on the utility stretcher, someone stuck his head back on because it wasn't off when I saw him. And plugged up the bullet-hole, and —"

"Rod, stop driveling," cut in the girl. "If you don't want to tell me, all right."

Rod grinned. "Don't get mad. Say, how's your father?"

"Lots better. He's asleep now and definitely on the up-grade. I think he'll be back at the university by next week. Rod, you look tired. When do those forms have to be in?"

"Twenty-four hours after the crime. But —"

"But nothing. Come on over here right now. You can make out those old forms in the morning."

She smiled at him, and Caquer weakened. He was not getting anywhere anyway, was he?

"All right, Jane," he said. "But I'm going by patrol quarters on the way. Had some men canvassing the block the crime was committed in, and I want their report."

But the report, which he found waiting for him, was not illuminating. The canvass had been thorough, but it had failed to elicit any information of value. No one had been seen to leave or enter the Deem shop prior to Bragers's arrival, and none of Deem's neighbors knew of any enemies he might have. No one had heard a shot.

Rod Caquer grunted and stuffed the reports into his pocket, and wondered, as he walked to the Gordon home, where the investigation went from here. How did a detective go about solving such a crime?

True, when he was a college kid back on Earth a few years ago, he had read that a detective usually trapped someone by discovering a discrepancy in his statements. Generally in a rather dramatic manner, too.

There was Wilder Williams, the greatest of all the fictional detectives, who could look at a man and deduce his whole life history from the cut of his clothes and the shape of his hands. But Wilder Williams had never run across a victim who had been killed in as many ways.

He spent a pleasant — but futile — evening with Jane Gordon, again asked her to marry him, and again was refused. But he was used to that. She was a bit cooler this evening than usual, probably because she resented his unwillingness to talk about Willem Deem.

And home, to bed.

Out the window of his apartment, after the light was out, he could see the monstrous ball of Jupiter hanging low in the sky, the green-black midnight sky. He lay in bed and stared at it until it seemed that he could still see it after he had closed his eyes.

Willem Deem, deceased. What was he going to do about Willem Deem? Around and around, until at last one orderly thought emerged from chaos.

Tomorrow morning he would talk to the medico. Without mentioning the sword wound in the head, he would ask Skidder about the bullet hole Brager claimed to have seen over the heart. If Skidder still said the blaster burn was the only wound, he would summon Brager and let him argue with the medico.

And then — well, he would worry about what to do then when he got there. He would never get to sleep this way.

He thought about Jane, and went to sleep.

After a while, he dreamed. Or was it a dream? If so, then he dreamed that he was lying there in bed, almost but not quite awake, and that there were whispers coming from all corners of the room. Whispers out of the darkness.

For big Jupiter had moved on across the sky now. The window was a dim, scarcely-discernible outline, and the rest of the room in utter darkness.

Whispers!

"— kill them."

"You hate them, you hate them, you hate them."

"— kill, kill, kill."

"Sector Two gets all the gravy and Sector Three does all the work. They exploit our corla plantations. They are evil. Kill them, take over."

"You hate them, you hate them, you hate them."

"Sector Two is made up of weaklings and usurers. They have the taint of Martian blood. Spill it, spill Martian blood. Sector Three should rule Callisto. Three the mystic number. We are destined to rule Callisto."

"You hate them, you hate them."

"— kill, kill, kill."

"Martian blood of usurious villains. You hate them, you hate them, you hate them."

Whispers.

"Now — now — now."

"Kill them, kill them."

"A hundred ninety miles across the flat planes. Get there in an hour in monocars. Surprise attack. Now. Now. Now."

And Rod Caquer was getting out of bed, fumbling hastily and blindly into his clothing without turning on the light because this was a dream and dreams were in darkness.

His sword was in the scabbard at his belt, and he took it out and felt the edge and the edge was sharp and ready to spill the blood of the enemy he was going to kill.

Now it was going to swing in arcs of red death, his un-blooded sword — the anachronistic sword that was his badge of office, of authority. He had never drawn the sword in anger, a stubby symbol of a sword, scarce eighteen inches long; enough, though, enough to reach the heart — four inches to the heart.

The whispers continued.

"You hate them, you hate them, you hate them."

"Spill the evil blood; kill, spill, kill, spill."

"Now, now, now, now."

Unsheathed sword in clenched fist, he was stealing silently out the door, down the stairway, past the other apartment doors.

And some of the doors were opening, too. He was not alone, there in the darkness. Other figures moved beside him in the dark.

He stole out of the door and into the night-cooled darkness of the street, the darkness of the street that should have been brightly lighted. That was another proof that this was a dream. Those streetlights were never off, after dark. From dusk till dawn, they were never off.

But Jupiter over there on the horizon gave enough light to see by. Like a round dragon in the heavens, and the red spot like an evil, malignant eye.

Whispers breathed in the night, whispers from all around him.

"Kill — kill — kill —"

"You hate them, you hate them, you hate them."

The whispers did not come from the shadowy figures about him. They pressed forward silently, as he did.

Whispers came from the night itself, whispers that now began to change tone.

"Wait, not tonight, not tonight, not tonight," they said.

"Go back, go back, go back."

"Back to your homes, back to your beds, back to your sleep."

And the figures about him were standing there, fully as irresolute as he had now become. And then, almost simultaneously, they began to obey the whispers. They turned back, and returned the way they had come, and as silently. . . .

Rod Caquer awoke with a mild headache and a hangover feeling. The sun, tiny but brilliant, was already well up in the sky.

His clock showed him that he was a bit later than usual, but he took time to lie there for a few minutes, just the same, remembering that screwy dream he'd had. Dreams were like that; you had to think about them right away when you woke up, before you were really fully awake, or you forgot them completely.

A silly sort of dream, it had been. A mad, purposeless, dream. A touch of atavism, perhaps? A throwback to the days when peoples had been at each other's throats half the time, back to the days of wars and hatreds and struggle for supremacy.

This was before the Solar Council, meeting first on one inhabited planet and then another, had brought order by arbitration, and then union. And now war was a thing of the past. The inhabitable portion of the solar system—Earth, Venus, Mars, and the moons of Jupiter—were all under one government.

But back in the old bloody days, people must have felt as he had felt in that atavistic dream. Back in the days when Earth, united by the discovery of space travel, had subjugated Mars — the only other planet already inhabited by an intelligent race — and then had spread colonies wherever Man could get a foothold.

Certain of those colonies had wanted independence and, next, supremacy. The bloody centuries, those times were called now.

Getting out of bed to dress, he saw something that puzzled and dismayed him. His clothing was not neatly folded over the back of the chair beside the bed as he had left it. Instead, it was strewn about the floor as though he had undressed hastily and carelessly in the dark.

Earth! he thought. *Did I sleepwalk last night? Did I actually get out of bed and go out into the street when I dreamed that I did? When those whispers told me to?*

No, he then told himself, *I've never walked in my sleep before, and I didn't then. I must simply have been careless when I undressed last night. I was thinking about the Deem case. I don't actually remember hanging my clothes on that, chair.*

So he donned his uniform quickly and hurried down to the office. In the light of morning it was easy to fill out those forms. In the "Cause of Death" blank he wrote, "Medical Examiner reports that shock from a blaster wound caused death."

That let him out from under; he had not said that was the cause of death; merely that the medico said it was.

CHAPTER III

Blackdex

He rang for a messenger and gave him the reports with instructions to rush them to the mail ship that would be leaving shortly. Then he called Barr Maxon.

"Reporting on the Deems matter, Regent," he said. "Sorry, but we just haven't got anywhere on it yet. Nobody was seen leaving the shop. All the neighbors have been questioned. Today I'm going to talk to all his friends."

Regent Maxon shook his head.

"Use all jets, Lieutenant," he said. "The case must be cracked. A murder, in this day and age, is bad enough. But an unsolved one is unthinkable. It would encourage further crime."

Lieutenant Caquer nodded gloomily. He had thought of that, too. There were the social implications of murder to be worried about — and there was his job as well. A Lieutenant of Police who let anyone get away with murder in his district was through for life.

After the Regent's image had clicked off the visiphone screen, Caquer took the list of Deem's friends from the drawer of his desk and began to study it, mainly with an eye to deciding the sequence of his calls.

He penciled a figure "1" opposite the name of Perry Peters for two reasons. Peters's place was only a few doors away, for one thing, and for another he knew Perry better than anyone on the list, except possibly Professor Jan Gordon. And he would make that call last, because later there would be a better chance of finding the ailing professor awake — and a better chance of finding his daughter Jane at home.

Perry Peters was glad to see Caquer, and guessed immediately the purpose of the call.

"Hello, Shylock."

"Huh?" said Rod.

"Shylock — the great detective. Confronted with a mystery for the first time in his career as a policeman. Or have you solved it, Rod?"

"You mean Sherlock, you dope — Sherlock Holmes. No, I haven't solved it, if you want to know. Look, Perry, tell me all you know about Deem. You knew him pretty well, didn't you?"

Perry Peters rubbed his chin reflectively and sat down on the work bench. He was so tall and lanky that he could sit down on it instead of having to jump up.

"Willem was a funny little runt," he said. "Most people didn't like him because he was sarcastic, and he had crazy notions on politics. Me, I'm not sure whether he wasn't half right half the time, and anyway he played a swell game of chess."

"Was that his only hobby?"

"No. He liked to make things, gadgets mostly. Some of them were good, too, although he did it for fun and never tried to patent or capitalize anything."

"You mean inventions, Perry? Your own line?"

"Well, not so much inventions as gadgets, Rod. Little things, most of them, and he was better on fine workmanship than on original ideas. And, as I said, it was just a hobby with him."

"Ever help you with any of your own inventions?" asked Caquer.

"Sure, occasionally. Again, not so much on the idea of it as by helping me make difficult parts." Perry Peters waved his hand in a gesture that included the shop around them. "My tools here are all for rough work, comparatively. Nothing under thousandths. But Willem has — had — a little lathe that's a honey. Cuts anything, and accurate to a fifty-thousandth."

"What enemies did he have, Perry?"

"None that I know of. Honestly, Rod. Lot of people disliked him, but just an ordinary mild kind of dislike. You know what I mean, the kind of dislike that makes 'em trade at another book-and-reel shop, but not the kind that makes them want to kill anybody."

"And who, as far as you know, might benefit by his death?"

"Um — nobody, to speak of," said Peters, thoughtfully. "I think his heir is a nephew on Venus. I met him once, and he was a likable guy. But the estate won't be anything to get excited about. A few thousand credits is all I'd guess it to be."

"Here's a list of his friends, Perry." Caquer handed Peters a paper. "Look it over, will you, and see if you can make any additions to it. Or any suggestions."

The lanky inventor studied the list, and then passed it back. "That includes them all, I guess," he told Caquer. "Couple on there I didn't know he knew well enough to rate listing. And you have his best customers down, too; the ones that bought heavily from him."

Lieutenant Caquer put the list back in his pocket.

"What are you working on now?" he asked Peters.

"Something I'm stuck on, I'm afraid," the inventor said. "I needed Deem's help — or at least the use of his lathe — to go ahead with this." He picked up from the bench a pair of the most peculiar-looking goggles Rod Caquer had ever seen. The lenses were shaped like arcs of circles instead of full circles, and they fastened in a band of resilient plastic obviously designed to fit close to the face above and below the lenses. At the top center, where it would be against the forehead of the goggles' wearer, was a small cylindrical box an inch and a half in diameter.

"What on Earth are they for?" Caquer asked.

"For use in radite mines. The emanations from that stuff, while it's in the raw state, destroys immediately any transparent substance yet made or discovered. Even quartz. And it isn't good on naked eyes, either. The miners have to work blindfolded, as it were, and by their sense of touch."

Rod Caquer looked at the goggles curiously.

"But how is the funny shape of these lenses going to keep the emanations from hurting them, Perry?" he asked.

"That part up on top is a tiny motor. It operates a couple of specially-treated wipers across the lenses. For all the world like an old-fashioned windshield wiper, and that's why the lenses are shaped like the wiper-arm arcs."

"Oh," said Caquer. "You mean the wipers are absorbent and hold some kind of liquid that protects the glass?"

"Yes, except that it's quartz instead of glass. And it's protected only a minute fraction of a second. Those wipers go like the devil — so fast you can't see them when you're wearing the goggles. The arms are half as big as the arcs, and the wearer can see out of only a fraction of the lens at a time. But he can see, dimly, and that's a thousand per cent improvement in radite mining."

"Fine, Perry," said Caquer. "And they can get around the dimness by having ultra-brilliant lighting. Have you tried these out?"

"Yes, and they work. Trouble's in the rods; friction heats them, and they expand and jam after it's run a minute, or thereabouts. I have to turn them down on Deem's lathe — or one like it. Think you could arrange for me to use it? Just for a day or so?"

"I don't see why not," Caquer told him. "I'll talk to whomever the Regent appoints executor and fix it up. And later you can probably buy the lathe from his heir. Or does the nephew go in for such things?"

Perry Peters shook his head. "Nope; he wouldn't know a lathe from a drill-press. Be swell of you, Rod, if you can arrange for me to use it."

Caquer had turned to go, when Perry Peters stopped him.

"Wait a minute," Peters said and then paused and looked uncomfortable. "I guess I was holding out on you, Rod," he said at last. "I do know one thing about Willem that might possibly have something to do with his death, although I don't see how, myself. I wouldn't tell it on him, except that he's dead, and so it won't get him in trouble."

"What was it, Perry?"

"Illicit political books. He had a little business on the side selling them. Books on the index — you know just what I mean."

Caquer whistled softly. "I didn't know they were made anymore. After the council put such a heavy penalty on them — whew!"

"People are still human, Rod. They still want to know the things they shouldn't know — just to find out why they shouldn't, if for no other reason."

"Graydex or Blackdex books, Perry?"

Now the inventor looked puzzled.

"I don't get it. What's the difference?"

"Books on the official index," Caquer explained, "are divided into two groups. The really dangerous ones are in the Blackdex. There's a severe penalty for owning one, and a death penalty for writing or printing one. The mildly dangerous ones are in the Graydex, as they call it."

"I wouldn't know which Willem peddled. Well, off the record, I read a couple Willem lent me once, and I thought they were pretty dull stuff. Unorthodox political theories."

"That would be Graydex." Lieutenant Caquer looked relieved. "Theoretical stuff is all Graydex. The Blackdex books are the ones with dangerous practical information."

"Such as?" The inventor was staring intently at Caquer.

"Instructions how to make outlawed things," explained Caquer. "Like Lethite, for instance. Lethite is a poison gas that's tremendously dangerous. A few pounds of it could wipe out a city, so the council outlawed its manufacture, and any book telling people how to make it for themselves would go on the Blackdex. Some nitwit might get hold of a book like that and wipe out his whole home town."

"But why would anyone?"

"He might he warped mentally and have a grudge," explained Caquer. "Or he might want to use it on a lesser scale for criminal reasons. Or — by Earth, he might be the head of a government with designs on neighboring states. Knowledge of a thing like that might upset the peace of the Solar System."

Perry Peters nodded thoughtfully. "I get your point," he

said. "Well, I still don't see what it could have to do with the murder, but I thought I'd tell you about Willem's sideline. You probably want to check over his stock before whoever takes over the shop reopens."

"We shall," said Caquer. "Thanks a lot, Perry. If you don't mind, I'll use your phone to get that search started right away. If there are any Blackdex books there, we'll take care of them all right."

When he got his secretary on the screen, she looked both frightened and relieved at seeing him.

"Mr. Caquer," she said, "I've been trying to reach you. Something awful's happened. Another death."

"Murder again?" gasped Caquer.

"Nobody knows what it was," said the secretary. "A dozen people saw him jump out of a window only twenty feet up. And in this gravity that couldn't have killed him, but he was dead when they got there. And four of them that saw him knew him. It was —"

"Well, for Earth's sake, who?"

"I don't — Lieutenant Caquer, they said, all four of them, that it was Willem Deem!"

CHAPTER IV

Rule of Thumb

With a nightmarish feeling of unreality Lieutenant Rod Caquer peered down over the shoulder of the Medico-in-Chief at the body that already lay on the stretcher of the utility men, who stood by impatiently.

"You better hurry, Doc," one of them said. "He won't last much longer, and it took us five minutes to get there."

Dr. Skidder nodded impatiently without looking up and went on with his examination. "Not a mark, Rod," he said. "Not a sign of poison. Not a sign of anything. He's just dead."

"The fall couldn't have caused it?" said Caquer.

"There isn't even a bruise from the fall. Only verdict I can give is heart failure. Okay, boys, you can take him away."

"You through too, Lieutenant?"

"I'm through," said Caquer. "Go ahead. Skidder, which of them was Willem Deem?"

The medico's eyes followed the white-sheeted burden of the utility men as they carried it toward the truck, and he shrugged helplessly.

"Lieutenant, I guess that's your pigeon," he said. "All I can do is certify to cause of death."

"It just doesn't make sense," Caquer wailed. "Sector Three City isn't so big that he could have had a double living here without people knowing about it. But one of them had to be a double. Off the record, which looked to you like the original?"

Dr. Skidder shook his head grimly.

"Willem Deem had a peculiarly shaped wart on his nose," he said. "So did both of *his* corpses, Rod. And neither one was artificial, or make-up. I'll stake my professional reputation on that. But come on back to the office with me, and I'll tell you which one of them is the real Willem Deem."

"Huh? How?"

"His thumbprint's on file at the tax department, like everybody's is. And it's part of routine to fingerprint a corpse on Callisto, because it has to be destroyed so quickly."

"You have thumbprints of both corpses?" inquired Caquer.

"Of course. Took them before you reached the scene, both times. I have the one for Willem — I mean the other corpse — back in my office. Tell you what — you pick up the print on file at the tax office and meet me there."

Caquer sighed with relief as he agreed. At least one point in the case would be cleared up — which corpse was which.

And in that comparatively blissful state of mind he remained until half an hour later when he and Dr. Skidder compared the time prints — the one Rod Caquer had secured from the tax office, and one from each of the corpses.

They were identical, all three of them.

"Um," said Caquer. "You're sure you didn't get mixed up on those prints, Dr. Skidder.

"How could I? I took only one copy from each body, Rod. If I had shuffled them just now while we were looking at them, the result would be the same. All three prints are alike."

"But they can't be."

Skidder shrugged.

"I think we should lay this before the Regent, direct," he said. "I'll call him and arrange an audience. Okay?"

Half an hour later, he was giving the whole story to Regent Barr Maxon, with Dr. Skidder corroborating the main points. The expression on Regent Maxon's face made Lieutenant Rod Caquer glad, very glad, that he had that corroboration.

"You agree," Maxon asked, "that this should be taken up with the Sector Coordinator, and that a special investigator should be sent here to take over?"

A bit reluctantly, Caquer nodded. "I hate to admit that I'm incompetent, Regent, or that I seem to be," Caquer said. "But this isn't an ordinary crime. Whatever goes on, it's way over my head. And there may be something even more sinister than murder behind it."

"You're right, Lieutenant. I'll see that a qualified man leaves headquarters today, and he'll get in touch with you in the morning."

"Regent," Caquer asked, "has any machine or process ever been invented that will — uh — duplicate a human body, with or without the mind being carried over?"

Maxon seemed puzzled by the question.

"You think Deem might have been playing around with something that bit him. No, to my knowledge a discovery like that has never been approached. Nobody has ever duplicated, except by constructive imitation, even an inanimate object. You haven't heard of such a thing, have you, Skidder?"

"No," said the Medical Examiner. "I don't think even your friend Perry Peters could do that, Rod."

From the Regent Maxon's office, Caquer went on Deem's shop. Brager was in charge there, and Brager helped him search the place thoroughly. It was a long and laborious task, because each book and reel had to be examined minutely.

The printers of illicit books, Caquer knew, were clever at disguising their product. Usually, forbidden books bore the cover and title page, often even the opening chapters, of some popular work of fiction, and the projection reels were similarly disguised.

Jupiter-lighted darkness was falling outside when they finished, but Rod Caquer knew they had done a thorough job. There wasn't an indexed book anywhere in the shop, and every reel had been run off on a projector.

Other men, at Rod Caquer's orders, had been searching Deem's apartment with equal thoroughness. He phoned there and got a report, completely negative.

"Not so much as a Venusian pamphlet," said the man in charge at the apartment, with what Caquer thought was a touch of regret in his voice.

"Did you come across a lathe, a small one for delicate work?" Rod asked.

"Um — no, we didn't see anything like that. One room's turned into a workshop, but there's no lathe in it. Is it important?"

Caquer grunted noncommittally. What was one more mystery, and a minor one at that, to a case like this?

"Well, Lieutenant," Brager said when the screen had gone blank. "What do we do now?"

Caquer sighed.

"You can go off duty, Brager," he said. "But first arrange to leave men on guard here and at the apartment. I'll stay until whoever you send comes to relieve me."

When Brager had left, Caquer sank wearily into the nearest chair. He felt terrible, physically, and his mind just did not seem to be working. He let his eyes run again around the orderly shelves of the shop, and their orderliness oppressed him.

If there was only a clue of some sort. Wilder Williams had never had a case like this in which the only leads were two identical corpses, one of which had been killed five different ways and the other did not have a mark or sign of violence. What a mess, and where did he go from here?

Well, he still had the list of people he was going to interview, and there was time to see at least one of them this evening.

Should he look up Perry Peters again and see what, if anything, the lanky inventor could make of the disappearance of the lathe? Perhaps he might be able to suggest what had happened to it. But then again, what could a lathe have to do with a mess like this? One cannot turn out a duplicate corpse on a lathe.

Or should he look up Professor Gordon? He decided to do just that.

He called the Gordon apartment on the visiphone, and Jane appeared in the screen.

"How's your father," Caquer asked Jane. "Will he be able to talk to me for a while this evening?"

"Oh, yes," said the girl. "He's feeling much better and thinks he'll go back to his classes tomorrow. But get here early if you're coming. Rod, you look terrible; what's the matter with you?"

"Nothing, except I feel goofy. But I'm all right, I guess."

"You have a gaunt, starved look. When did you eat last?"

Caquer's eyes widened. "Earth! I forgot all about eating. I slept late and didn't even have breakfast!"

Jane Gordon laughed.

"You dope! Well, hurry around, and I'll have something ready for you when you get here."

"But —"

"But nothing. How soon can you start?"

"Soon."

A minute after he had clicked off the visiphone, Lieutenant Caquer went to answer a knock on the shuttered door of the shop.

He opened it. "Oh, hullo, Reese," he said. "Did Brager send you?"

The policeman nodded.

"He said I was to stay here in case. In case what?"

"Routine guard duty, that's all," explained Caquer. "Say, I've been stuck here all afternoon. Anything going on?"

"A little excitement. We been pulling in soap-box orators off and on all day. Screwballs. There's an epidemic of them."

"The devil you say! What are they hipped about?"

"Sector Two, for some reason I can't make out. They're trying to incite people to get mad at Sector Two and do something about it. The arguments they use are plain nutty."

Something stirred uneasily in Rod Caquer's memory, but he could not quite remember what it was. Sector Two? Who'd been telling him things about Sector Two recently — usury, unfairness, tainted blood, something silly. Although of course a lot of the people over there did have Martian blood in them . . .

"How many of the orators were arrested?" he asked.

"We got seven. Two more slipped away from us, but we'll pick them up if they start spouting that kind of stuff again."

L ieutenant Caquer walked slowly, thoughtfully, to the Gordon apartment, trying his level best to remember where, recently, he heard anti-Sector Two propaganda. There must be something back of the simultaneous appearance of nine soapbox radicals, all preaching the same doctrine.

A sub-rosa political organization? But none such had existed for almost a century now. Under a perfectly democratic government, component part of a stable system-wide organization of planets, there was no need for such activity. Of course an occasional crackpot was dissatisfied, but a group in that state of mind struck him as fantastic.

It sounded as crazy as the Willem Deem case. That did not make sense either. Things happened meaninglessly, as in a dream.

Dream? What was he trying to remember about a dream? Hadn't he had an odd sort of dream last night — what was it?

But, as dreams usually do, it eluded his conscious mind.

Anyway, tomorrow he would question — or help question — those radicals who were under arrest. Put men on the job of tracing them, and undoubtedly a common background somewhere, a tie-up, would be found.

It could not be accidental that they should all pop up on the same day. It was screwy, just as screwy as the two inexplicable corpses of a book-and-reel shop proprietor. Maybe because the cases were both screwy, his mind tended to couple the two sets of events. But taken together, they were no more digestible than taken separately. They made even less sense.

Confound it, why hadn't he taken that post on Ganymede when it was offered to him? Ganymede was a nice orderly moon. Persons there did not get murdered twice on consecutive days. But Jane Gordon did not live on Ganymede; she lived right here in Sector Three, and he was on his way to see her.

And everything was wonderful except that he felt so tired he could not think straight, and Jane Gordon insisted on looking on him as a brother instead of a suitor, and he was probably going to lose his job. He would be the laughingstock of Callisto if the special investigator from headquarters found some simple explanation of things that he had overlooked. . . .

CHAPTER V

Nine-Man Morris

Jane Gordon, looking more beautiful than he had ever seen her, met him at the door. She was smiling, but the smile changed to a look of concern as he stepped into the light.

"Rod!" she exclaimed. "You do look ill, really ill. What have you been doing to yourself besides forgetting to eat?"

Rod Caquer managed a grin.

"Chasing vicious circles up blind alleys, Icicle. May I use your visiphone?"

"Of course. I've some food ready for you; I'll put it on the table while you're calling. Dad's taking a nap. He said to wake him when you got here, but I'll hold off until you're fed."

She hurried out to the kitchen. Caquer almost fell into the chair before the visiscreen and called the police station. The red, beefy face of Borgesen, the night lieutenant, flashed into view.

"Hi, Borg," said Caquer. "Listen, about those seven screw-balls you picked up. Have you —"

"Nine," Borgesen interrupted. "We got the other two, and I wish we hadn't. We're going nuts down here."

"You mean the other two tried it again?"

"No. Suffering asteroids, they came in and gave themselves up, and we can't kick them out because there's a charge against them. But they're confessing all over the place. And do you know what they're confessing?"

"I'll bite," said Caquer.

"That you hired them and offered one hundred credits apiece to them."

"Huh?"

Borgesen laughed, a little wildly. "The two that came in voluntarily say that, and the other seven — Gosh, why did I ever become a policeman? I had a chance to study for fireman on a spacer once, and I end up doing this."

"Look — maybe I better come around and see if they make that accusation to my face."

"They probably would, but it doesn't mean anything, Rod. They say you hired them this afternoon, and you were at Deem's with Brager all afternoon. Rod, this moon is going nuts. And so am I. Walter Johnson has disappeared. Hasn't been seen since this morning."

"What? The Regent's confidential secretary? You're kidding me, Borg."

"Wish I was. You ought to be glad you're off duty. Maxon's been raising seven brands of thunder for us to find his secretary for him. He doesn't like the Deem business, either. Seems to blame us for it; thinks it's bad enough for the department to let a man get killed once. Say, which was Deem, Rod? Got any idea?"

Caquer grinned weakly.

"Let's call them Deem and Redeem till we find out," he suggested. "I think they were both Deem."

"But how could one man be two?"

"How could one man be killed five ways?" countered Caquer. "Tell me that and I'll tell you the answer to yours."

"Nuts," said Borgesen, and followed it with a masterpiece of understatement. "There's something funny about that case."

Caquer was laughing so hard that there were tears in his eyes when Jane Gordon came to tell him food was ready. She frowned at him, but there was concern behind the frown.

Caquer followed her meekly and discovered he was ravenous. When he'd put himself outside enough food for three ordinary meals, he felt almost human again. His headache was still there, but it was something that throbbed dimly in the distance.

Frail Professor Gordon was waiting in the living room when they went there from the kitchen.

"Rod, you look like something the cat dragged in," he said. "Sit down before you fall down."

Caquer grinned. "Overeating did it. Jane's a cook in a million."

He sank into a chair facing Gordon. Jane sat on the arm of her father's chair, and Caquer's eyes feasted on her. How could a girl with lips as soft and kissable as hers insist on regarding marriage only as an academic subject? How could a girl with —

"I don't see offhand how it could be a cause of his death, Rod; but Willem Deem rented out political books," said Gordon. "There's no harm in my telling that, since the poor chap is dead."

Almost the same words, Caquer remembered, that Perry Peters had used in telling him the same thing. Caquer nodded.

"We've searched his shop and his apartment and haven't found any, Professor," he said. "You wouldn't know, of course, what kind —"

Professor Gordon smiled. "I'm afraid I would, Rod. Off the record — and I take it you haven't a recorder on our conversation — I've read quite a few of them."

"You?" There was frank surprise in Caquer's voice.

"Never underestimate the curiosity of an educator, my boy. I fear the reading of Graydex books is a more prevalent vice among the instructors in universities than among any other class. Oh, I know it's wrong to encourage the trade, but the reading of such books can't possibly harm a balanced, judicious mind."

"And Father certainly has a balanced, judicious mind, Rod," said Jane, a bit defiantly., "Only — darn him — he wouldn't let me read those books."

Caquer grinned at her. The professor's use of the word "Graydex" had reassured him. Renting Graydex books was only a misdemeanor, after all.

"Ever read any Graydex books, Rod?" the professor asked.

Caquer shook his head.

"No."

"Then you've probably never heard of hypnotism. Some of the circumstances in the Deem case — well, I've wondered whether hypnotism might have been used."

"I'm afraid I don't even know what it is, Professor."

The frail little man sighed. "That's because you've never read illicit books, Rod," said Gordon. "Hypnotism is the control of one mind by another, and it reached a pretty high state of development before it was outlawed. You've never heard of the Kaprelian Order or the Vargas Wheel?"

Caquer shook his head.

"The history of the subject is in Graydex books, in several of them," said the professor. "The actual methods, and how a Vargas Wheel is constructed, would be Blackdex, high on the roster of the lawlessness. Of course, I haven't read that, but I have read the history.

"A man by the name of Mesmer, way back in the Eighteenth Century, was one of the first practitioners, if not the discoverer, of hypnotism. At any rate, he put it on a more or less scientific basis. By the twentieth century, quite a bit had been learned about it — and it became extensively used in medicine.

"A hundred years later, doctors were treating almost as many patients through hypnotism as through drugs and surgery. True, there were cases of its misuse, but they were relatively few.

"But another hundred years brought a big change. Mesmerism had developed too far for the public safety. Any criminal or selfish politician who had a smattering of the art could operate with impunity. He could fool all the people all the time and get away with it."

"You mean he could really make people think anything he wanted them to?" Caquer asked.

"Not only that, he could make them do anything he wanted. And by that time, television was in such common use that one speaker could visibly and directly talk to millions of people."

"But couldn't the government have regulated the art?"

Professor Gordon smiled thinly. "How, when legislators were human, too, and as subject to hypnotism as the people under them? And then, to complicate things almost hopelessly, came the invention of the Vargas Wheel.

"It had been known, back as far as the nineteenth century, that an arrangement of moving mirrors could throw anyone who watched it into a state of hypnotic submission. And thought transmission had been experimented with in the twenty-first century. It was in the following one that Vargas combined and perfected the two into the Vargas Wheel. A sort of helmet affair, really, with a revolving wheel of specially constructed tricky mirrors on top of it."

"How did it work, Professor?" asked Caquer.

"The wearer of a Vargas Wheel helmet had immediate and automatic control over anyone who saw him — directly, or in a television screen," said Gordon. "The mirrors in the small, turning wheel produced instantaneous hypnosis and the helmet — somehow — brought thoughts of its wearer to bear through the wheel and impressed upon his subjects any thoughts he wished to transmit.

"In fact, the helmet itself — or the wheel — could be set to produce certain fixed illusions without the necessity of the operator speaking, or even concentrating, on those points. Or the control could be direct, from his mind."

"Ouch," said Caquer. "A thing like that would — I can certainly see why instructions in making a Vargas Wheel would be Blackdexed. Suffering Asteroids! A man with one of these could —"

"Could do almost anything. Including killing a man and making the manner of his death appear five different ways to five different observers."

Caquer whistled softly. "And including playing nine-man Morris with soapbox radicals — or they wouldn't even have to be radicals. They could be ordinary orthodox citizens."

"Nine men?" Jane Gordon demanded. "What's this about nine men, Rod? I hadn't heard about it."

But Rod was already standing up.

"Haven't time to explain, Icicle," he said. "Tell you tomorrow, but I must get down to — wait a minute. Professor, is that all you know about the Vargas Wheel business?"

"Absolutely all, my boy. It just occurred to me as a possibility. There were only five or six of them ever made, and finally the government got hold of them and destroyed them, one by one. It cost millions of lives to do it.

"When they finally got everything cleaned up, colonization of the planets was starting, and an international council had been started with control over all governments. They decided that the whole field of hypnotism was too dangerous, and they made it a forbidden subject. It took quite a few centuries to wipe out all knowledge of it, but they succeeded. The proof is that you'd never heard of it."

"But how about the beneficial aspects of it," Jane Gordon asked. "Were they lost?"

"Of course," said her father. "But the science of medicine had progressed so far by that time that it wasn't too much of a loss. Today the medicos can cure, by physical treatment, anything that hypnotism could handle."

Caquer, who had halted at the door, now turned back.

"Professor, do you think it possible that someone could have rented a Blackdex book from Deem and learned all those secrets?" he inquired.

Professor Gordon shrugged. "It's possible," he said. "Deem might have handled occasional Blackdex books, but he knew better than try to sell or rent any to me. So I wouldn't have heard of it."

A t the station, Lieutenant Caquer found Lieutenant Borgesen on the verge of apoplexy. He looked at Caquer.

"You!" he said. And then, plaintively, "The world's gone nuts. Listen, Brager discovered Willem Deem, didn't he? At ten o'clock yesterday morning? And stayed there on guard while Skidder and you and the clearance men were there?"

"Yes, why?" asked Caquer.

Borgesen's expression showed how much he was upset by developments.

"Nothing, not a thing, except that Brager was in the emergency hospital yesterday morning, from nine until after eleven, getting a sprained ankle treated. He couldn't have been at Deem's. Seven doctors and attendants and nurses swear up and down he was in the hospital at that time."

Caquer frowned.

"He was limping today, when he helped me search Deem's shop," he said. "What does Brager say?"

"He says he was there, I mean at Deem's, and discovered Deem's body. We just happened to find out otherwise accidentally — if it is otherwise. Rod, I'm going nuts. To think I had a chance to be fireman on a spacer and took this celestial job. Have you learned anything new?"

"Maybe. But first I want to ask you, Borg. About these nine nitwits you picked up. Has anybody tried to identify —"

"Them," interrupted Borgesen. "I let them go."

Caquer stared at the beefy face of the night lieutenant in utter amazement.

"Let them go?" he repeated. "You couldn't, legally. Man, they'd been charged. Without a trial, you couldn't turn them loose."

"Nuts. I did, and I'll take the responsibility for it. Look, Rod, they were right, weren't they?"

"What?"

"Sure. People ought to be waked up about what's going on over in Sector Two. Those phonies over there need taking down a peg, and we're the only ones to do it. This ought to be headquarters for Callisto, right here. Why, listen, Rod, a united Callisto could take over Ganymede."

"Borg, was there anything over the televis tonight? Anybody make a speech you listened to?"

"Sure, didn't you hear it? Our friend Skidder. Must have been while you were walking here, because all the televis turned on automatically — it was a general."

"And — was anything specific suggested, Borg? About Sector Two, and Ganymede, and that sort of thing?"

"Sure, general meeting tomorrow morning at ten. In the square. We're all supposed to go; I'll see you there, won't I?"

"Yeah," said Lieutenant Caquer. "I'm afraid you will. I — I got to go, Borg."

CHAPTER VI

Too Familiar Face

Ron Caquer knew what was wrong now. Also the last thing he wanted to do was stay around the station listening to Borgesen talking under the influence of what seemed to be a Vargas Wheel. Nothing else, nothing less, could have made police Lieutenant Borgesen talk as he had just talked. Professor Gordon's guess was getting righter every minute. Nothing else could have brought about such results.

Caquer walked on blindly through the Jupiter-lighted night, past the building in which his own apartment was. He did not want to go there either.

The streets of Sector Three City seemed crowded for so late an hour of the evening. Late? He glanced at his watch and whistled softly. It was not evening any more. It was two o'clock in the morning, and normally the streets would have been utterly deserted.

But they were not, tonight. People wandered about, alone or in small groups that walked together in uncanny silence. Shuffle of feet, but not even the whisper of a voice. Not even whispers! Something about those streets and the people on them made Rod Caquer remember, now, his dream of the night before. Only now he knew that it had not been a dream. Nor had it been sleepwalking, in the ordinary sense of the word.

He had dressed. He had stolen out of the building. And the street lights had been out too, and that meant that employees of the service department had neglected their posts. They, like others, had been wandering with the crowds.

"Kill — kill — kill — You hate them. . . ."

A shiver ran down Rod Caquer's spine as he realized the significance of the fact that last night's dream had been a reality. This was something that dwarfed into insignificance the murder of a petty book-and-reel shop owner. This was something which was gripping a city, something that could upset a world, something that could lead to unbelievable terror and carnage on a scale that hadn't been known since the twenty-fourth century. This — which had started as a simple murder case!

Up ahead somewhere, Rod Caquer heard the voice of a man addressing a crowd. A frenzied voice, shrill with fanaticism. He hurried his steps to the corner and walked around it to find himself in the fringe of a crowd of people pressing around a man speaking from the top of a flight of steps.

"— and I tell you that tomorrow is the day. Now we have the Regent himself with us, and it will be unnecessary to depose him. Men are working all night tonight, preparing. After the meeting in the square tomorrow morning, we shall —"

"Hey!" Rod Caquer yelled. The man stopped talking and turned to look at Rod, and the crowd turned slowly, almost as one man, to stare at him.

"You're under —"

Then Caquer saw that this was but a futile gesture.

It was not because of the man surging toward him that convinced him of this. He was not afraid of violence. He would have welcomed it as relief from uncanny terror, welcomed a chance to lay about him with the flat of his sword.

But standing behind the speaker was a man in uniform — Brager. And Caquer remembered, then, that Borgesen, now in charge at the station, was on the other side. How could he arrest the speaker when Borgesen, now in charge, would refuse to book him. And what good would it do to start a riot and cause injury to innocent people — people acting not under their own volition, but under the insidious influence Professor Gordon had described to him?

Hand on his sword, he backed away. No one followed. Like automatons, they turned back to the speaker, who resumed his harangue as though never interrupted. Policeman Brager had not moved, had not even looked in the direction of his superior officer. He alone of all those there had not turned at Caquer's challenge.

Lieutenant Caquer hurried on in the direction he had been going when he had heard the speaker. That way would take him back downtown. He would find a place open where he could use a visiphone and call the Sector Coordinator. This was an emergency. And surely the scope of whoever had the Vargas Wheel had not yet extended beyond the boundaries of Sector Three.

He found an all-night restaurant, open but deserted, the lights on but no waiters on duty, no cashier behind the counter. He stepped into the visiphone booth and pushed the button for a long-distance operator. She flashed into sight on the screen almost at once.

"Sector Coordinator, Callisto City," Caquer said. "And rush it."

"Sorry, sir. Out of town service suspended by order of the Controller of Utilities, for the duration."

"Duration of what?"

"We are not permitted to give out information."

Caquer gritted his teeth. Well, there was one someone who might be able to help him. He forced his voice to remain calm.

"Give me Professor Gordon, University Apartments," he told the operator.

"Yes, sir."

But the screen stayed dark, although the little red button that indicated the buzzer was operating flashed on and off, for minutes.

"There is no answer, sir."

Probably Gordon and his daughter were asleep, too soundly asleep to hear the buzzer. For a moment, Caquer considered rushing over there. But it was on the other side of town, and of what help could they be? None, and Professor Gordon was a frail old man, and ill. No, he would have to —

Again he pushed a button of the visiphone and a moment later was talking to the man in charge of the ship hangar.

"Get out that little speed job of the Police Department,"

snapped Caquer. "Have it ready and I'll be there in a few minutes."

"Sorry, Lieutenant," came the curt reply. "All outgoing power beams shut off, by special order. Everything is grounded for the emergency."

He might have known it, Caquer thought. But what about the special investigator coming in from the Coordinator's office?

"Are incoming ships still permitted to land?" he inquired.

"Permitted to land, but not to leave again without special order," answered the voice.

"Thanks," Caquer said. He clicked off the screen and went outside into the dawn. There was a chance, then. The special investigator might be able to help.

But he, Rod Caquer would have to intercept him, tell him the story and its implications before he could fall, with the others, under the influence of the Vargas Wheel. Caquer strode rapidly toward the terminal. Maybe it was too late. Maybe his ship had already landed and the damage had been done.

Again he passed a knot of people gathered about a frenzied speaker. Almost everyone must be under the influence by this time. But why had he been spared? Why was not he, too, under the evil influence?

True, he must have been on the street on the way to the police station at the time Skidder had been on the air, but that didn't explain everything. All of these people could not have seen and heard that visicast. Some of them must have been asleep already at that hour.

Also he, Rod Caquer, had been affected, the night before, the night of the whispers. He must have been under the influence of the wheel at the time he investigated the murder — the murders.

Why, then, was he free now? Was he the only one, or were there others who had escaped, who were sane and their normal selves?

If not, if he was the only one, why was he free? Or *was* he free? Could it be that what he was doing right now was under direction, was part of some plan?

But no use to think that way and go mad. He would have to carry on the best he could and hope that things, with him, were what they seemed to be.

Then he broke into a run, for ahead was the open area of the terminal, and a small spaceship, silver in the dawn, was settling down to land. A small official speedster — it must he the special investigator. He ran around the check-in building, through the gate in the wire fence and toward the ship, which was already down, the door opening.

A small, wiry man stepped out and closed the door behind him. He saw Caquer and smiled.

"You're Caquer?" he asked pleasantly. "Coordinator's office sent me to investigate a case you fellows are troubled with. My name —"

Lieutenant Rod Caquer was staring with horrified fascination at the little man's well-known features, the all-too-familiar wart on the side of the little man's nose, listening for the announcement he knew this man was going to make

"— is Willem Deem. Shall we go to your office?"

CHAPTER VII
Wheels Within the Wheel

Such a thing as too much can happen to any man! Lieutenant Rod Caquer, Lieutenant of Police of Sector Three, Callisto, had experienced more than his share. How can you investigate the murder of a man who has been killed twice? How should a policeman act when the victim shows up, alive and happy, to help you solve the case?

Not even when you know he is not there really — or if he is, he is not what your eyes tell you he is and is not saying what your ears hear.

There is a point beyond which the human mind can no

longer function sanely with proper sense as when they reach and pass that point, different people react in different ways.

Rod Caquer's reaction was a sudden blind, red anger. Directed, for lack of a better object, at the special investigator — if he was the special investigator and not a hypnotic phantasm which wasn't there at all.

Rod Caquer's fist lashed out, and it met a chin. Which proved nothing except that if the little man who'd just stepped out of the speedster was an illusion, he was an illusion of touch as well as of sight. Rod's fist exploded on his chin like a rocket-blast, and the little man swayed and fell forward. Still smiling, because he had not had time to change the expression on his face.

He fell face down, and then rolled over, his eyes closed but smiling gently up at the brightening sky.

Shakily, Caquer bent down and put his hand against the front of the man's tunic. There was the thump of a beating heart, all right. For a moment, Caquer had feared he might have killed with that blow.

And Caquer closed his eyes, deliberately, and felt the man's face with his hand — and it still felt like the face of Willem Deem looked, and the wart was there to the touch as well as to the sense of sight.

Two men had run out of the check-in building and were coming across the field toward him. Rod caught the expression on their faces and then thought of the little speedster only a few paces from him. He had to get out of Sector Three City, to tell somebody what was happening before it was too late. If only they'd been lying about the outgoing power beam being shut off. He leaped across the body of the man he had struck and into the door of the speedster, jerked at the controls. But the ship did not respond, and no, they hadn't been lying about the power beam.

No use staying here for a fight that could not possibly decide anything. He went out the door of the speedster, on the other side, away from the men coming toward him, and ran for the fence.

It was electrically charged, that fence. Not enough to kill a man, but plenty to hold him stuck to it until men with rubber gloves cut the wire and took him off. But if the power beam was off, probably the current in the fence was off, too.

It was too high to jump, so he took the chance. And the current was off. He scrambled over it safely, and his pursuers stopped and went back to take care of the fallen man beside the speedster.

Caquer slowed down to a walk, but he kept on going. He didn't know where, but he had somehow to keep moving. After a while he found that his steps were taking him toward the edge of town, on the northern side, toward Callisto City.

But that was silly. He couldn't possibly walk to Callisto City and get there in less than three days. Even if he could walk across the intervening roadless desert at all. Besides, three days would be too late.

He was in a small park near the north border when the significance, and the futility, of his direction came to him. And he found, at the same time, that his muscles were sore and tired, that he had a raging headache, that he could not keep on going unless he had a worthwhile and possible goal.

He sat down on a park bench, and for a while his head was sunk in his hands. No answer came.

After a while, he looked up and saw something that fascinated him. A child's pinwheel on a stick, stuck in the grass of the park, spinning in the wind. Now fast, now slow, as the breeze varied.

It was going in circles, like his mind was. How could a man's mind go other than in circles when he could not tell what was reality and what was illusion? Going in circles, like a Vargas Wheel.

Circles.

But there ought to be some way. A man with a Vargas Wheel was not completely invincible, else how had the council finally succeeded in destroying the few that had been made? True, possessors of the wheels would have cancelled each other out to some extent, but there must have been a last wheel in someone's hands. Owned by someone who wanted to control the destiny of the solar system.

But they had stopped the wheel.

It could be stopped, then. But how? How, when one could not see it? Rather, when the sight of it put a man so completely under its control that he no longer, after the first glimpse, knew that it was there because, on sight, it had captured his mind.

He must stop the wheel. That was the only answer. But how?

That pinwheel there could be the Vargas Wheel, for all he could tell, set to create the illusion that it was a child's toy. Or its possessor, wearing the helmet, might be standing on the path in front of him at this moment, watching him. The possessor of the wheel might be invisible because Caquer's mind was told not to see.

But if the man was there, he'd be really there, and should Rod slash out with his sword, the menace would be ended, wouldn't it? Of course.

But how to find a wheel that one could not see? That one could not see because—

And then, still staring at the pinwheel, Caquer saw a chance, something that might work, a slender chance!

He looked quickly at his wrist watch and saw that it was half past nine, which was one half hour before the demonstration in the square. And the wheel and its owner would be there, surely.

His aching muscles forgotten, Lieutenant Rod Caquer started to run back toward the center of town. The streets were deserted. Everyone had gone to the square, of course. They had been told to come.

He was winded after a few blocks and had to slow down to a rapid walk, but there would be time for him to get there before it was over, even if he missed the start.

Yes, he could get there all right. And then, if his idea worked . . .

It was almost ten when he passed the building where his

own office was situated, and kept on going. He turned in a few doors beyond. The elevator operator was gone, but Caquer ran the elevator up, and a minute later he had used his picklock on a door and was in Perry Peters's laboratory.

Peters was gone, of course, hut the goggles were there, the special goggles with the trick windshield-wiper effect that made them usable in radite mining.

Rod Caquer slipped them over his eyes, put the motive-power battery into his pocket, and touched the button on the side. They worked. He could see dimly as the wipers flashed back and forth. But a minute later they stopped.

Of course. Peters had said that the shafts heated and expanded after a minute's operation. Well, that might not matter. A minute might be long enough, and the metal would have cooled by the time he reached the square.

But he would have to be able to vary the speed. Among the litter of stuff on the workbench, he found a small rheostat and spliced it in one of the wires that ran from the battery to the goggles.

That was the best he could do. No time to try it out. He slid the goggles up onto his forehead and ran out into the hall, took the elevator down to street level. And a moment later he was running toward the public square, two blocks away.

He reached the fringe of the crowd gathered in the square looking up at the two balconies of the Regency building. On the lower one were several people he recognized; Dr. Skidder, Walther Johnson. Even Lieutenant Borgesen was there.

On the higher balcony, Regent Maxon Barr was alone and was speaking to the crowd below. His sonorous voice rolled out phrases extolling the might of empire. Only a little distance away, in the crowd, Caquer caught sight of the gray hair of Professor Gordon, and Jane Gordon's golden head beside it. He wondered if they were under the spell, too. Of course they were deluded also or they would not be there. He realized it would be useless to speak to them, then, and tell them what he was trying to do.

Lieutenant Caquer slid the goggles down over his eyes, blinded momentarily because the wiper arms were in the *wrong* position. But his fingers found the rheostat, set at zero, and began to move it slowly around the dial toward maximum.

And then, as the wipers began their frantic dance and accelerated, he could see dimly. Through the arc-shaped lenses, he looked around him. On the lower balcony he saw nothing unusual, but on the upper balcony the figure of Regent Barr suddenly blurred.

There was a man standing there on the upper balcony wearing a strange-looking helmet with wires, and atop the helmet was a three-inch wheel of mirrors and prisms. For an instant, the speed of those wiper arms was synchronized with the spinning of the wheel, so that each successive glimpse of the wheel showed it in the same position, and to Caquer's eyes the wheel stood still, and he could see it.

Then the goggles jammed.

But he did not need them any more now.

He knew that Barr Maxon, or whoever stood up there on the balcony, was the wearer of the wheel.

Silently, and attracting as little attention as possible, Caquer sprinted around the fringe of the crowd and reached the side door of the Regency building.

There was a guard on duty there.

"Sorry, sir, but no one's allowed —" Then he tried to duck, too late. The flat of Police Lieutenant Rod Caquer's short-sword thudded against his head.

The inside of the building seemed deserted. Caquer ran up the three flights of stairs that would take him to the level of the higher balcony and down the hall toward the balcony door.

He burst through it, and Regent Maxon turned. Maxon now, no longer wore the helmet on his head. Caquer had lost the goggles, but whether he could see it or not, Caquer knew the helmet and the wheel were still in place and working, and that this was his one chance.

Maxon turned and saw Lieutenant Caquer's face, and his drawn sword.

Then, abruptly, Maxon's figure vanished. It seemed to Caquer — although he knew that it was not — that the figure before him was that of Jane Gordon. Jane, looking at him pleadingly, spoke in melting tones.

"Rod, don't —" she began to say.

But it was not Jane, he knew. A thought, in self-preservation, had been directed at him by the manipulator of the Vargas Wheel.

Caquer raised his sword, and he brought it down hard.

Glass shattered, and there was the ring of metal on metal as his sword cut through and split the helmet.

Of course it was not Jane now — just a dead man lying there with blood oozing out of the split in a strange and complicated, but utterly shattered, helmet. A helmet that could now be seen by everyone there, and by Lieutenant Caquer himself.

Just as everyone, including Caquer, himself, could recognize the man who had worn it.

He was a small, wiry man, and there was an unsightly wart on the side of his nose.

Yes, it was Willem Deem. And this time, Rod Caquer knew, it *was* Willem Deem. . . .

"I thought," Jane Gordon said, "that you were going to leave for Callisto City without saying goodbye to us."

Rod Caquer threw his hat in the general direction of a hook. "Oh, that," he said. "I'm not even sure I'm going to take the promotion to a job as police coordinator there. I have a week to decide, and I'll he around town at least that long. How you been doing, Icicle?"

"Fine, Rod. Sit down. Father will be home soon, and I know he has a lot of things to ask you. Why, we haven't seen you since the big mass meeting."

Funny how dumb a smart man can be, at times. But then

again, he had proposed so often and been refused, that it was not all his fault.

He just looked at her.

"Rod, all the story never came out in the newscasts," she said. "I know you'll have to tell it all over again for my father, but while we're waiting for him, won't you give me some information?"

Rod grinned.

"Nothing to it, really, Icicle," he said. "Willem Deem got hold of a Blackdex book and found out how to make a Vargas Wheel. So he made one, and it gave him ideas.

"His first idea was to kill Barr Maxon and take over as Regent, setting the helmet so he would appear to be Maxon. He put Maxon's body in his own shop, and then had a lot of fun with his own murder. He had a warped sense of humor, and got a kick out of chasing us in circles."

"But just how did he do all the rest?" asked the girl.

"He was there as Brager, and pretended to discover his own body. He gave one description of the method of death, and caused Skidder and me and the clearance men to see the body of Maxon each a different way. No wonder we nearly went nuts."

"But Brager remembered being there too," she objected.

"Brager was in the hospital at the time, but Deem saw him afterward and impressed on his mind the memory pattern of having discovered Deem's body," explained Caquer. "So naturally, Brager thought he had been there.

"Then he killed Maxon's confidential secretary because, being so close to the Regent, the secretary must have suspected something was wrong even though he couldn't guess what. That was the second corpse of Willem Deem, who was beginning to enjoy himself in earnest when he pulled that on us.

"And of course he never sent to Callisto City for a special investigator at all. He just had fun with me, by making me seem to meet one and having the guy turn out to be Willem Deem again. I nearly did go nuts then, I guess."

"But why, Rod, weren't you as deeply in as the others — I mean on the business of conquering Callisto and all of that?" she inquired. "You were free of that part of the hypnosis."

Caquer shrugged.

"Maybe it was because I missed Skidder's talk on the televis," he suggested. "Of course, it wasn't Skidder at all, it was Deem in another guise and wearing the helmet. And maybe he deliberately left me out, because he was having a psychopathic kind of fun out of my trying to investigate the murders of two Willem Deems. It's hard to figure. Perhaps I was slightly cracked from the strain, and it might have been that for that reason I was partially resistant to the group hypnosis."

"You think he really intended to try to rule all of Callisto, Rod?" asked the girl.

"We'll never know, for sure, just how far he wanted, or expected to go later. At first, he was just experimenting with the powers of hypnosis through the wheel. That first night, he sent people out of their houses into the streets, and then sent them back and made them forget it. Just a test, undoubtedly."

Caquer paused and frowned thoughtfully.

"He was undoubtedly psychopathic, though, and we don't dare even guess what all his plans were," he continued. "You understand how the goggles worked to neutralize the wheel, don't you, Icicle?"

"I think so. That was brilliant, Rod. It's like when you take a moving picture of a turning wheel, isn't it? If the camera synchronizes with the turning of the wheel, so that each successive picture shows it after a complete revolution, then it looks like it's standing still when you show the movie."

Caquer nodded.

"That's it on the head," he said. "Just luck I had access to those goggles, though. For just a second I could see a man wearing a helmet up there on the balcony — but that was all I had to know."

"But Rod, when you rushed out on the balcony, you

didn't have the goggles on any more. Couldn't he have stopped you by hypnosis?"

"Well, he didn't. I guess there wasn't time for him to take over control of me. He did flash an illusion at me. It wasn't either Barr Maxon or Willem Deem I saw standing there at the last minute. It was you, Jane."

"I?"

"Yep, you. I guess he knew I'm in love with you, and that's the first thing that popped into his mind; that I wouldn't dare use the sword if I thought it was you standing there. But I knew it wasn't you, in spite of the evidence of my eyes, so I swung it."

He shuddered slightly, remembering the will power he had needed to bring that blade down.

"The worst of it was that I saw you standing there like I've always wanted to see you — with your arms out toward me, and looking at me as though you loved me."

"Like this, Rod?"

And he was not too dumb to get the idea this time.

THE LITTLE LAMB

She didn't come home for supper, and by eight o'clock I found some ham in the refrigerator and made myself a sandwich. I wasn't worried, but I was getting restless. I kept walking to the window and looking down the hill toward town, but I couldn't see her coming. It was a moonlit evening, very bright and clear. The lights of the town were nice and the curve of the hills beyond, black against blue under a yellow gibbous moon. I thought I'd like to paint it, but not the moon; you put a moon in a picture and it looks corny, it looks pretty. Van Gogh did it in his picture "The Starry Sky," and it didn't look pretty; it looked frightening, but then again he was crazy when he did it; a sane man couldn't have done many of the things Van Gogh did.

I hadn't cleaned my palette so I picked it up and tried to work a little more on the painting I'd started the day before. It was just blocked in thus far, and I started to mix a green to fill in an area, but it wouldn't come right, and I realized I'd have to wait till daylight to get it right. Evenings, without natural light, I can work on line or I can mold in finishing strokes, but when color's the thing, you've got to have daylight. I cleaned my messed-up palette for a fresh start in the morning, and I cleaned my brushes, and it was getting close to nine o'clock, and still she hadn't come.

No, there wasn't anything to worry about. She was with friends somewhere, and she was all right. My studio is almost a mile from town, up in the hills; and there wasn't any way she could let me know because there's no phone. Probably she was having a drink with the gang at the Waverly Inn, and there was no reason she'd think I'd worry about her. Neither of us lived by the clock; that was understood between us. She'd be home soon.

There was half of a jug of wine left; and I poured myself a drink and sipped it, looking out the window toward town. I turned off the light behind me so I could better watch out the window at the bright night. A mile away, in the valley, I could see the lights of the Waverly Inn. Garish bright, like the loud jukebox that kept me from going there often. Strangely, Lamb never minded the jukebox, although she liked good music, too.

Other lights dotted here and there. Small farms, a few other studios. Hans Wagner's place a quarter of a mile down the slope from mine. Big, with a skylight; I envied him that skylight. But not his strictly academic style. He'd never paint anything quite as good as a color photograph; in fact, he saw things as a camera sees them and painted them without filtering them through the catalyst of the mind. A wonderful draftsman, never more. But his stuff sold; he could afford a skylight.

I sipped the last of my glass of wine, and there was a tight knot in the middle of my stomach. I didn't know why. Often Lamb had been later than this, much later. There wasn't any real reason to worry.

I put my glass down on the windowsill and opened the door. But before I went out, I turned the lights back on. A beacon for Lamb, if I should miss her. And if she should look up the hill toward home and the lights were out, she might think I wasn't there and stay longer, wherever she was. She'd know I wouldn't turn in before she got home, no matter how late it was.

Quit being a fool, I told myself; it isn't late yet. It's early, just past nine o'clock. I walked down the hill toward town and the knot in my stomach got tighter and I swore at myself because there was no reason for it. The line of the hills beyond town rose higher as I descended, pointing up the stars. It's difficult to make stars that look like stars. You'd have to make pinholes in the canvas and put a light behind it. I laughed at the idea — but why not? Except that it isn't done, and what did I care about that. But I thought awhile, and I saw why it wasn't done. It would be childish, immature.

I was about to pass Hans Wagner's place, and I slowed my steps thinking that just possibly Lamb might be there. Hans lived alone there and Lamb wouldn't, of course, be there unless a crowd had gone to Hans's from the inn or somewhere. I stopped to listen and there wasn't a sound, so the crowd wasn't there. I went on.

The road branched; there were several ways from here and I might miss her. I took the shortest route, the one she'd be most likely to take if she came directly home from town. It went past Carter Brent's place, but that was dark. There was a light on at Sylvia's place, though, and guitar music. I knocked on the door, and while I was waiting I realized that it was the phonograph and not a live guitarist. It was Segovia playing Bach, the Chaconne from the D-Minor Partita, one of my favorites. Very beautiful, very fine-boned and delicate, like Lamb.

Sylvia came to the door and answered my question. No, she hadn't seen Lamb. And no, she hadn't been at the inn, or anywhere. She'd been home all afternoon and evening, but did I want to drop in for a drink? I was tempted — more by Segovia than by the drink — but I thanked her and went on.

I should have turned around and gone back home instead, because for no reason I was getting into one of my black moods. I was illogically annoyed because I didn't know where Lamb was; if I found her now I'd probably quarrel with her, and I hate quarreling. Not that we do, often. We're each pretty tolerant and understanding — of little things, at least. And Lamb's not having come home yet was still a little thing.

But I could hear the blaring jukebox when I was still a long way from the inn, and it didn't lighten my mood any. I could see in the window now and Lamb wasn't there, not at the bar. But there were still the booths, and besides, someone might know where she was. There were two couples at the bar. I knew them: Charlie and Eve Chandler, and Dick Bristow with a girl from Los Angeles whom I'd met but whose name I couldn't remember. And one fellow, stag, who looked as though he was trying to look like a movie scout from Hollywood. Maybe he really was one.

I went in and, thank God, the jukebox stopped just as I went through the door. I went over to the bar, glancing at the line of booths; Lamb wasn't there.

I said, "Hi," to the four of them that I knew, and to the stag if he wanted to take it to cover him, and to Harry, behind the bar. "Has Lamb been here?" I asked Harry.

"Nope, haven't seen her, Wayne. Not since six; that's when I came on. Want a drink?"

I didn't, particularly; but I didn't want it to look as though I'd come solely for Lamb, so I ordered one.

"How's the painting coming?" Charlie Chandler asked me.

He didn't mean any particular painting and he wouldn't have known anything about it if he had. Charlie runs the local bookstore and — amazingly — he can tell the difference between Thomas Wolfe and a comic book, but he couldn't tell the difference between an El Greco and an Al Capp. Don't misunderstand me on that; I like Al Capp.

So I said, "Fine," as one always says to a meaningless question, and took a swallow of the drink that Harry had put in front of me. I paid for it and wondered how long I'd have to stay in order to make it not too obvious that I'd come only to look for Lamb.

For some reason, conversation died. If anybody had been talking to anybody before I came in, he wasn't now. I glanced at Eve and she was making wet circles on the mahogany of the bar with the bottom of a martini goblet. The olive stirred restlessly in the bottom and I knew suddenly that was the color, the exact color I'd wanted to mix an hour or two ago just before I'd decided not to try to paint. The color of an olive moist with gin and vermouth. Just right for the main sweep of the biggest hill, shading darker to the right, lighter to the left. I stared at the color and memorized it so I'd have it tomorrow. Maybe I'd even try it tonight when I got back home; I had it now, daylight or no. It was right; it was the color that had to be there. I felt good; the black mood that had threatened to come on was gone.

But where was Lamb? If she wasn't home yet when I got back, would I be able to paint? Or would I start worrying about her, without reason? Would I get that tightness in the pit of my stomach?

I saw that my glass was empty. I'd drunk too fast. Now I might as well have another one, or it would be too obvious why I'd come. And I didn't want people — not even people like these — to think I was jealous of Lamb and worried about her. Lamb and I trusted each other implicitly. I was curious as to where she was and I wanted her back, but that was all. I wasn't suspicious of where she might be. They wouldn't realize that.

I said, "Harry, give me a martini." I'd had so few drinks that it wouldn't hurt me to mix them, and I wanted to study that color, intimately and at close hand. It was going to be the central color motif; everything would revolve around it.

Harry handed me the martini. It tasted good. I swished around the olive and it wasn't quite the color I wanted, a little too much in the brown, but I still had the idea. And I still wanted to work on it tonight, if I could find Lamb. If she was there, I could work; I could get the planes of color in, and tomorrow I could mode them, shade them.

But unless I'd missed her, unless she was already home or on her way there, it wasn't too good a chance. We knew dozens of people; I couldn't try every place she might possibly be. But there was one other fairly good chance, Mike's Club, a mile down the road, out of town on the other side. She'd hardly have gone there unless she was with someone who had a car, but that could have happened. I could phone there and find out.

I finished my martini and nibbled the olive and then turned around to walk over to the phone booth. The wavy-haired man who looked as though he might be from Hollywood was just walking back toward the bar from the juke-box, and it was making preliminary scratching noises. He'd dropped a coin into it, and it started to play something loud and brassy. A polka, and a particularly noisy and obnoxious one. I felt like hitting him one in the nose, but I couldn't even catch his eye as he strolled back and took his stool again at the bar. And anyway, he wouldn't have known what I was hitting him for. But the phone booth was just past the jukebox and I wouldn't hear a word, or be heard, if I phoned Mike's.

A record takes about three minutes, and I stood one minute of it and that was enough. I wanted to make that call and get out of there, so I walked toward the booth and I reached around the jukebox and pulled the plug out of the wall. Quietly, not violently at all. But the sudden silence was violent, so violent that I could hear, as though she'd screamed them, the last few words of what Eve Chandler had been saying to Charlie Chandler. Her voice pitched barely to carry above the din of brass — but she might as well have used a public address system once I'd pulled the jukebox's plug.

"— may be at Hans's." Bitten off suddenly, as if she'd intended to say more.

Her eyes met mine and hers looked frightened.

I looked back at Eve Chandler. I didn't pay any attention to Golden Boy from Hollywood; if he wanted to make anything of the fact that I'd ruined his dime, that was his business and he could start it. I went into the phone booth and pulled the door shut. If that jukebox started again before I'd finished my call, it would be my business, and I could start it. The jukebox didn't start again.

I gave the number of Mike's, and when someone answered, I asked, "Is Lamb there?"

"Who did you say?"

"This is Wayne Gray," I said patiently. "Is Lambeth Gray there?"

"Oh." I recognized it now as Mike's voice. "Didn't get you at first. No, Mr. Gray, your wife hasn't been here."

I thanked him and hung up. When I went out of the booth, the Chandlers were gone. I heard a car starting outside.

I waved to Harry and went outside. The taillight of the Chandlers' car was heading up the hill. In the direction they'd have gone if they were heading for Hans Wagner's studio — to warn Lamb that I'd heard something I shouldn't have heard, and that I might come there.

But it was too ridiculous to consider. Whatever gave Eve Chandler the wild idea that Lamb might be with Hans, it was wrong. Lamb wouldn't do anything like that. Eve had probably seen her having a drink or so with Hans somewhere, sometime, and had got the thing wrong. Dead wrong. If nothing else, Lamb would have better taste than that. Hans was handsome, and he was a ladies' man, which I'm not, but he's stupid and he can't paint. Lamb wouldn't fall for a stuffed shirt like Hans Wagner.

But I might as well go home now, I decided. Unless I wanted to give people the impression that I was canvassing the town for my wife, I couldn't very well look any farther or ask any more people if they'd seen her. And although I don't care what people think about me either personally or as a painter, I wouldn't want them to think I had any wrong ideas about Lamb.

I walked off in the wake of the Chandlers' car, through the bright moonlight. I came in sight of Hans's place again, and the Chandlers' car wasn't parked there; if they'd stopped, they'd gone right on. But, of course, they would have, under those circumstances. They wouldn't have wanted me to see that they were parked there; it would have looked bad.

The lights were on there, but I walked on past, up the hill toward my own place. Maybe Lamb was home by now; I hoped so. At any rate, I wasn't going to stop at Hans's. Whether the Chandlers had or not.

Lamb wasn't in sight along the road between Hans's place and mine. But she could have made it before I got that far, even if — well, even if she had been there. If the Chandlers had stopped to warn her.

Three quarters of a mile from the inn to Hans's. Only one quarter of a mile from Hans's place to mine. And Lamb could have run; I had only walked.

Past Hans's place, a beautiful studio with that skylight I

envied him. Not the place, not the fancy furnishings, just that wonderful skylight. Oh, yes, you can get wonderful light outdoors, but there's wind and dust just at the wrong time. And when, mostly, you paint out of your head instead of something you're looking at, there's no advantage to being outdoors at all. I don't have to look at a hill while I'm painting it. I've seen a hill.

The light was on at my place, up ahead. But I'd left it on, so that didn't prove Lamb was home. I plodded toward it, getting a little winded by the uphill climb, and I realized I'd been walking too fast. I turned around to look back and there was that composition again, with the gibbous moon a little higher, a little brighter. It had lightened the black of the near hills and the far ones were blacker. I thought, *I can do that.* Gray on black and black on gray. And, so it wouldn't be a monochrome, the yellow lights. Like the lights at Hans's place. Yellow lights like Hans's yellow hair. Tall, Nordic-Teutonic type, handsome. Nice planes in his face. Yes, I could see why women liked him. Women, but not Lamb.

I had my breath back and started climbing again. I called out Lamb's name when I got near the door, but she didn't answer. I went inside, but she wasn't there.

The place was very empty. I poured myself a glass of wine and went over to look at the picture I'd blocked out. It was all wrong; it didn't mean anything. The lines were nice but they didn't mean anything at all. I'd have to scrape the canvas and start over. Well, I'd done that before. It's the only way you get anything, to be ruthless when something's wrong. But I couldn't start it tonight.

The tin clock said it was a quarter to eleven; still, that wasn't late. But I didn't want to think so I decided to read a while. Some poetry, possibly. I went over to the bookcase. I saw Blake, and that made me think of one of his simplest and best poems, "The Lamb." It had always made me think of Lamb — "Little lamb, who made thee?" It had always given me, personally, a funny twist to the line, a connotation that Blake, of course, hadn't intended. But I didn't want to read

Blake tonight. T.S. Eliot: "Midnight shakes the memory as a madman shakes a dead geranium." But it wasn't midnight yet, and I wasn't in the mood for Eliot. Not even Prufrock: "Let us go then, you and I, when the evening is spread out against the sky like a patient etherized upon a table —" He could do things with words that I'd have liked to do with pigments, but they aren't the same things, the same medium. Painting and poetry are as different as eating and sleeping. But both fields can be, and are, so wide. Painters can differ as greatly as Bonnard and Braque, yet both be great. Poets as great as Eliot and Blake. "Little lamb, who —" I didn't want to read.

And enough of thinking. I opened the trunk and got my forty-five caliber automatic. The clip was full; I jacked a cartridge into the chamber and put the safety catch on. I put it into my pocket and went outside. I closed the door behind me and started down the hill toward Hans Wagner's studio.

I wondered, had the Chandlers stopped there to warn them? Then either Lamb would have hurried home — or, possibly, she might have gone on with the Chandlers, to their place. She could have figured that to be less obvious than rushing home. So, even if she wasn't there, it would prove nothing. If she was, it would show that the Chandlers hadn't stopped there.

I walked down the road, and I tried to look at the crouching black beast of the hills, the yellow of the lights. But they added up to nothing; they meant nothing. Unfeeling, ungiving-to-feel, like a patient etherized upon a table. Damn Eliot, I thought; the man saw too deeply. The useless striving of the wasteland for something a man can touch but never have, the shaking of a dead geranium. As a madman. Little Lamb. Her dark hair and her darker eyes in the whiteness of her face. And the slender, beautiful whiteness of her body. The softness of her voice and the touch of her hands running through my hair. And Hans Wagner's hair, yellow as that mocking moon.

I knocked on the door. Not loudly, not softly, just a knock. Was it too long before Hans came?

Did he look frightened? I didn't know. The planes of his face were nice, but what was in them I didn't know. I can see the lines and the planes of faces, but I can't read them. Nor voices.

"Hi, Wayne. Come in," Hans said.

I went inside. Lamb wasn't there, not in the big room, the studio. There were other rooms, of course; a bedroom, a kitchen, a bathroom. I wanted to go look in all of them right away, but that would have been crude. I wouldn't leave until I'd looked in each.

"Getting a little worried about Lamb: she's seldom out alone this late. Have you seen her?" I asked.

Hans shook his blond, handsome head.

"Thought she might have dropped in on her way home," I said casually. I smiled at him. "Maybe I was just getting lonesome and restless. How about dropping back with me for a drink? I've got only wine, but there's plenty of that."

Of course he had to say, "Why not have a drink here?" He said it. He even asked me what I wanted, and I said a martini because he'd have to go out into the kitchen to make that and it would give me a chance to look around.

"Okay, Wayne, I'll have one too," Hans said. "Excuse me a moment."

He went out into the kitchen. I took a quick look into the bathroom and then went into the bedroom and took a good look, even under the bed. Lamb wasn't there. Then I went into the kitchen and said, "Forgot to tell you, make mine light. I might want to paint a bit after I get home."

"Sure," he said.

Lamb wasn't in the kitchen. Nor had she left after I'd knocked or come in; I remember Hans's kitchen door; it's pretty noisy and I hadn't heard it. And it's the only door aside from the front one.

I'd been foolish.

Unless, of course, Lamb had been here and had gone away with the Chandlers when they'd dropped by to warn them, if they had dropped by.

I went back into the big studio with the skylight and wandered around for a minute looking at the things on the walls. They made me want to puke, so I sat down and waited. I'd stay at least a few minutes to make it look all right. Hans came back.

He gave me my drink and I thanked him. I sipped it while he waited patronizingly. Not that I minded that. He made money and I didn't. But I thought worse of him than he could possibly think of me.

"How's your work going, Wayne?"

"Fine," I said. I sipped my drink. He'd taken me at my word and made it weak, mostly vermouth. It tasted lousy that way. But the olive in it looked darker, more the color I'd had in mind. Maybe, just maybe, with the picture built around that color, it would work out.

"Nice place, Hans," I said. "That skylight. I wish I had one."

He shrugged. "You don't work from models anyway, do you? And outdoors is outdoors."

"Outdoors is in your mind," I said. "There isn't any difference." And then I wondered why I was talking to somebody who wouldn't know what I was talking about. I wandered over to the window — the one that faced toward my studio — and looked out of it. I hoped I'd see Lamb on the way there, but I didn't. She wasn't here. Where was she? Even if she'd been here and left when I'd knocked, she'd have been on the way now. I'd have seen her.

I turned. "Were the Chandlers here tonight?" I asked him.

"The Chandlers? No; haven't seen them for a couple of days." He'd finished his drink. "Have another?" he asked.

I started to say no. I didn't. My eyes happened, just happened, to light on a closet door. I'd seen inside it once; it wasn't deep, but it was deep enough for a man to stand inside it. Or a woman.

"Thanks, Hans. Yes."

I walked over and handed him my glass. He went out into the kitchen with the glasses. I walked quietly over to the closet door and tried it.

It was locked.

And there wasn't a key in the door. That didn't make sense. Why would anyone keep a closet locked when he always locked all the outer doors and windows when he left?

Little lamb, who made thee?

Hans came out of the kitchen, a martini in each hand. He saw my hand on the knob of the closet door.

For a moment he stood very still and then his hands began to tremble; the martinis, his and mine, slopped over the rims and made little droplets falling to the floor.

I asked him, pleasantly, "Hans, do you keep your closet locked?"

"Is it locked? No, I don't, ordinarily." And then he realized he hadn't quite said it right, and he said, more fearlessly. "What's the matter with you, Wayne?"

"Nothing," I said. "Nothing at all." I took the forty-five out of my pocket. He was far enough away so that, big as he was, he couldn't think about trying to jump me.

I smiled at him instead. "How's about letting me have the key?"

More martini glistened on the tiles. These tall, big, handsome blonds, they haven't guts; he was scared stiff. He tried to make his voice normal. "I don't know where it is. What's wrong?"

"Nothing," I said. "But stay where you are. Don't move, Hans."

He didn't. The glasses shook, but the olives stayed in them. Barely. I watched him, but I put the muzzle of the big forty-five against the keyhole. I slanted it away from the center of the door so I wouldn't kill anybody who was hiding inside. I did that out of the corner of my eye, watching Hans Wagner.

I pulled the trigger. The sound of the shot, even in that big studio, was deafening, but I didn't take my eyes off Hans. I may have blinked.

I stepped back as the closet door swung slowly open. I lined the muzzle of the forty-five against Hans's heart. I kept it there as the door of the closet swung slowly toward me.

An olive hit the tiles with a sound that wouldn't have been audible, ordinarily. I watched Hans while I looked into the closet as the door swung fully open.

Lamb was there. Naked.

I shot Hans and my hand was steady, so one shot was enough. He fell with his hand moving toward his heart but not having time to get there. His head hit the tiles with a crushing sound. The sound was the sound of death.

I put the gun back into my pocket and my hand was trembling now.

Hans's easel was near me, his palette knife lying on the ledge.

I took the palette knife in my hand and cut my Lamb, my naked Lamb, out of her frame. I rolled her up and held her tightly; no one would ever see her thus. We left together and, hand in hand, started up the hill toward home. I looked at her in the bright moonlight. I laughed, and she laughed, but her laughter was like silver cymbals, and my laughter was like dead petals shaken from a madman's geranium.

Her hand slipped out of mine; and she danced, a white slim wraith.

Back over her shoulder her laughter tinkled and she said, "Remember, darling? Remember that you killed me when I told you about Hans and me? Don't you remember killing me this afternoon? Don't you, darling? Don't you remember?"

THE GEEZENSTACKS

One of the strange things about it was that Aubrey Walters wasn't at all a strange little girl. She was quite as ordinary as her father and mother, who lived in an apartment on Otis Street, and who played bridge one night a week, went out somewhere another night, and spent the other evenings quietly at home.

Aubrey was nine, and had rather stringy hair and freckles; but at nine one never worries about such things. She got along quite well in the not-too-expensive private school to which her parents sent her, she made friends easily and readily with other children, and she took lessons on a three-quarter-size violin and played it abominably.

Her greatest fault, possibly, was her predeliction for staying up late of nights, and that was the fault of her parents, really, for letting her stay up and dressed until she felt sleepy and wanted to go to bed. Even at five and six, she seldom went to bed before ten o'clock in the evening. And if, during a period of maternal concern, she was put to bed earlier, she never went to sleep anyway. So why not let the child stay up?

Now, at nine years, she stayed up quite as late as her parents did, which was about eleven o'clock of ordinary nights and later when they had company for bridge, or went out for the evening. Then it was later, for they usually took her along. Aubrey enjoyed it, whatever it was. She'd sit still as a mouse in a seat at the theater, or regard them with little-girl seriousness over the rim of a glass of ginger ale while they had a cocktail or two at a night club. She took the noise and the music and the dancing with big-eyed wonder and enjoyed every minute of it.

Sometimes Uncle Richard, her mother's brother, went along with them. She and Uncle Richard were good friends. It was Uncle Richard who gave her the dolls.

"Funny thing happened today," he'd said. "I'm walking down Rodgers Place, past the Mariner Building — you know,

Edith; it's where Doc Howard used to have his office — and something thudded on the sidewalk right behind me. And I turned around, and there was this package."

"This package" was a white box a little larger than a shoebox, and it was rather strangely tied with gray ribbon. Sam Walters, Aubrey's father, looked at it curiously.

"Doesn't look dented," he said. "Couldn't have fallen out of a very high window. Was it tied up like that?"

"Just like that. I put the ribbon back on after I opened it and looked in. Oh, I don't mean I opened it then or there. I just stopped and looked up to see who'd dropped it — thinking I'd see somebody looking out of a window. But nobody was, and I picked up the box. It had something in it, not very heavy, and the box and the ribbon looked like — well, not like something somebody'd throw away on purpose. So I stood looking up, and nothing happened, so I shook the box a little and —"

"All right, all right," said Sam Walters. "Spare us the blow-by-blow. You didn't find out who dropped it?"

"Right. And I went up as high as the fourth floor, askingthe people whose windows were over the place where I picked it up. They were all home, as it happened, and none of them had ever seen it. I thought it might have fallen off a window ledge. But —"

"What's in it, Dick?" Edith asked.

"Dolls. Four of them. I brought them over this evening for Aubrey. If she wants them."

He untied the package, and Aubrey said, "Oooo, Uncle Richard. They're — they're lovely."

Sam said, "Hm. Those look almost more like manikins than dolls, Dick. The way they're dressed, I mean. Must have cost several dollars apiece. Are you sure the owner won't turn up?"

Richard shrugged. "Don't see how he can. As I told you, I went up four floors, asking. Thought from the look of the box and the sound of the thud, it couldn't have come from even that high. And after I opened it, well — look —" He picked up one of the dolls and held it out for Sam Walters's inspection.

"Wax. The heads and hands, I mean. And not one of them cracked. It couldn't have fallen from higher than the second story. Even then, I don't see how —" He shrugged again.

"They're the Geezenstacks," said Aubrey.

"Huh?" Sam asked.

"I'm going to call them the Geezenstacks," Aubrey said. "Look, this one is Papa Geezenstack and this one is Mama Geezenstack, and the little girl one — that's — that's Aubrey Geezenstack. And the other man one, we'll call him Uncle Geezenstack. The little girl's uncle."

Sam chuckled. "Like us, eh? But if Uncle — uh — Geezenstack is Mama Geezenstack's brother, like Uncle Richard is Mama's brother, then his name wouldn't be Geezenstack."

"Just the same, it is," Aubrey said. "They're all Geezenstacks. Papa, will you buy me a house for them?"

"A doll house? Why —" He'd started to say, "Why, sure," but caught his wife's eye and remembered. Aubrey's birthday was only a week off and they'd been wondering what to get her. He changed it hastily to "Why, I don't know. I'll think about it."

It was a beautiful doll house. Only one-story high, but quite elaborate, and with a roof that lifted off so one could rearrange the furniture and move the dolls from room to room. It scaled well with the manikins Uncle Richard had brought.

Aubrey was rapturous. All her other playthings went into eclipse and the doings of the Geezenstacks occupied most of her waking thoughts.

It wasn't for quite a while that Sam Walters began to notice, and to think about, the strange aspect of the doings of the Geezenstacks. At first, with a quiet chuckle at the coincidences that followed one another.

And then, with a puzzled look in his eyes.

It wasn't until quite a while later that he got Richard off into a corner. The four of them had just returned from a play. He said, "Uh — Dick."

"Yeah, Sam?"

"These dolls, Dick. Where did you get them?"

Richard's eyes stared at him blankly. "What do you mean, Sam? I told you where I got them."

"Yes, but — you weren't kidding, or anything? I mean, maybe you bought them for Aubrey, and thought we'd object if you gave her such an expensive present, so you — uh —"

"No, honest, I didn't."

"But dammit, Dick, they couldn't have fallen out of a window, or dropped out, and not broken. They're wax. Couldn't someone walking behind you — or going by in an auto or something —?"

"There wasn't anyone around, Sam. Nobody at all. I've wondered about it myself. But if I was lying, I wouldn't make up a screwy story like that, would I? I'd just say I found them on a park bench or a seat in a movie. But why are you curious?"

"I — uh — I just got to wondering."

Sam Walters kept on wondering, too.

They were little things, most of them. Like the time Aubrey had said, "Papa Geezenstack didn't go to work this morning. He's in bed, sick."

"So?" Sam had asked. "And what is wrong with the gentleman?"

"Something he ate, I guess."

And the next morning, at breakfast, "And how is Mr. Geezenstack, Aubrey?"

"A little better, but he isn't going to work today yet, the doctor said. Tomorrow, maybe."

And the next day, Mr. Geezenstack went back to work. That, as it happened, was the day Sam Walters came home feeling quite ill, as a result of something he'd eaten for lunch. Yes, he'd missed two days from work. The first time he'd missed work on account of illness in several years.

And some things were quicker than that, and some slower. You couldn't put your finger on it and say, "Well, if this happens to the Geezenstacks, it will happen to us in twenty-four hours." Sometimes it was less than an hour. Sometimes as long as a week.

"Mama and Papa Geezenstack had a quarrel today."

And Sam had tried to avoid that quarrel with Edith, but it seemed he just couldn't. He'd been quite late getting home, through no fault of his own. It had happened often, but this time Edith took exception. Soft answers failed to turn away wrath, and at last he'd lost his own temper.

"Uncle Geezenstack is going away for a visit." Richard hadn't been out of town for years, but the next week he took a sudden notion to run down to New York. "Pete and Amy, you know. Got a letter from them asking me —"

"When?" Sam asked, almost sharply. "When did you get a letter?"

"Yesterday."

"Then last week you weren't — This sounds like a silly question, Dick, but last week were you thinking about going anywhere? Did you say anything to — to anyone about the possibility of your visiting someone?"

"Lord, no. Hadn't even thought about Pete and Amy for months, till I got their letter yesterday. Want me to stay a week."

"You'll be back in three days — maybe," Sam had said. He wouldn't explain, even when Richard did come back in three days. It sounded just too damn' silly to say that he'd known how long Richard was going to be gone, because that was how long Uncle Geezenstack had been away.

Sam Walters began to watch his daughter, and to wonder. She, of course, was the one who made the Geezenstacks do whatever they did. Was it possible that Aubrey had some strange preternatural insight which caused her, unconsciously, to predict things that were going to happen to the Walters and to Richard?

He didn't, of course, believe in clairvoyance. But was Aubrey clairvoyant?

"Mrs. Geezenstack's going shopping today. She's going to buy a new coat."

That one almost sounded like a put-up job. Edith had smiled at Aubrey and then looked at Sam. "That reminds me, Sam. Tomorrow I'll be downtown, and there's a sale at —"

"But, Edith, these are war times. And you don't need a coat."

He'd argued so earnestly that he made himself late for work. Arguing uphill, because he really could afford the coat and she really hadn't bought one for two years. But he couldn't explain that the real reason he didn't want her to buy one was that Mrs. Geezen— Why, it was too silly to say, even to himself.

Edith bought the coat.

Strange, Sam thought, that nobody else noticed those coincidences. But Richard wasn't around all the time, and Edith — well, Edith had the knack of listening to Aubrey's prattle without hearing nine-tenths of it.

"Aubrey Geezenstack brought home her report card to-day, Papa. She got ninety in arithmetic and eighty in spelling and —"

And two days later, Sam was calling up the headmaster of the school. Calling from a pay station, of course, so nobody would hear him. "Mr. Bradley, I'd like to ask a question that I have a — uh — rather peculiar, but important, reason for asking. Would it be possible for a student at your school to know in advance exactly what grades —"

No, not possible. The teachers themselves didn't know, until they'd figured averages, and that hadn't been done until the morning the report cards were made out, and sent home. Yes, yesterday morning, while the children had their play period.

"Sam," Richard said, "you're looking kind of seedy. Business worries? Look, things are going to get better from now on, and with your company, you got nothing to worry about anyway."

"That isn't it, Dick. It — I mean, there isn't anything I'm worrying about. Not exactly. I mean —" And he'd had to wriggle out of the cross-examination by inventing a worry or two for Richard to talk him out of.

He thought about the Geezenstacks a lot. Too much. If only he'd been superstitious, or credulous, it might not have been so bad. But he wasn't. That's why each succeeding coincidence hit him a little harder than the last.

Edith and her brother noticed it, and talked about it when Sam wasn't around.

"He has been acting queer lately, Dick. I'm — I'm really worried. He acts so — Do you think we could talk him into seeing a doctor or a —"

"A psychiatrist? Um, if we could. But I can't see him doing it, Edith. Something's eating him, and I've tried to pump him about it, but he won't open up. Y'know — I think it's got something to do with those damn dolls."

"Dolls? You mean Aubrey's dolls? The ones you gave her?"

"Yes, the Geezenstacks. He sits and stares at the doll house. I've heard him ask the kid questions about them, and he was serious. I think he's got some delusion or something about them. Or centering on them."

"But, Dick, that's — awful."

"Look, Edie, Aubrey isn't as interested in them as she used to be, and — Is there anything she wants very badly?"

"Dancing lessons. But she's already studying violin and I don't think we can let her —"

"Do you think if you promised her dancing lessons if she gave up those dolls, she'd be willing? I think we've got to get them out of the apartment. And I don't want to hurt Aubrey, so —"

"Well — but what would we tell Aubrey?"

"Tell her I know a poor family with children who haven't any dolls at all. And — I think she'll agree, if you make it strong enough."

"But, Dick, what will we tell Sam? He'll know better than that."

"Tell Sam, when Aubrey isn't around, that you think she's

getting too old for dolls, and that — tell him she's taking an unhealthy interest in them, and that the doctor advises — That sort of stuff."

Aubrey wasn't enthusiastic. She was not as engrossed in the Geezenstacks as she'd been when they were newer, but couldn't she have both the dolls and the dancing lessons?

"I don't think you'd have time for both, honey. And there are those poor children who haven't any dolls to play with, and you ought to feel sorry for them."

And Aubrey weakened, eventually. Dancing school didn't open for ten days, though, and she wanted to keep the dolls until she could start her lessons. There was argument, but to no avail.

"That's all right, Edie," Richard told her. "Ten days is better than not at all, and — well, if she doesn't give them up voluntarily, it'll start a rumpus and Sam'll find out what we're up to. You haven't mentioned anything to him at all, have you?"

"No. But maybe it would make him feel better to know they were —"

"I wouldn't. We don't know just what it is about them that fascinates or repels him. Wait till it happens, and then tell him. Aubrey has already given them away. Or he might raise some objection or want to keep them. If I get them out of the place first, he can't."

"You're right, Dick. And Aubrey won't tell him, because I told her the dancing lessons are going to be a surprise for her father, and she can't tell him what's going to happen to the dolls without telling the other side of the deal."

"Swell, Edith."

It might have been better if Sam had known. Or maybe everything would have happened just the same, if he had.

Poor Sam. He had a bad moment the very next evening. One of Aubrey's friends from school was there, and they were playing with the doll house. Sam watching them, trying to look less interested than he was. Edith was knitting and Richard, who had just come in, was reading the paper.

Only Sam was listening to the children and heard the suggestion.

"— and then let's have a play funeral, Aubrey. Just pretend one of them is —"

Sam Walters let out a sort of strangled cry and almost fell getting across the room.

There was a bad moment, then, but Edith and Richard managed to pass it off casually enough, outwardly. Edith discovered it was time for Aubrey's little friend to leave, and she exchanged a significant glance with Richard and they both escorted the girl to the door.

Whispered, "Dick, did you see —"

"Something is wrong, Edie. Maybe we shouldn't wait. After all, Aubrey has agreed to give them up, and —"

Back in the living room, Sam was still breathing a bit hard. Aubrey looked at him almost as though she was afraid of him. It was the first time she'd ever looked at him like that, and Sam felt ashamed. He said, "Honey, I'm sorry I — But listen, you'll promise me you'll never have a play funeral for one of your dolls? Or pretend one of them is badly sick or has an accident — or anything bad at all? Promise?"

"Sure, Papa. I'm — I'm going to put them away for tonight."

She put the lid on the doll house and went back toward the kitchen.

In the hallway, Edie said, "I'll — I'll get Aubrey alone and fix it with her. You talk to Sam. Tell him — look, let's go out tonight, go somewhere and get him away from everything. See if he will."

Sam was still staring at the doll house.

"Let's get some excitement, Sam," Richard said. "How's about going out somewhere? We've been sticking too close to home. It'll do us good."

Sam took a deep breath. "Okay, Dick. If you say so. I — I could use a little fun, I guess."

Edie came back with Aubrey, and she winked at her brother. "You men go on downstairs and get a cab from the stand around the corner. Aubrey and I'll be down by the time you bring it."

Behind Sam's back, as the men were putting on their coats, Richard gave Edith an inquiring look and she nodded.

Outside, there was a heavy fog; one could see only a few yards ahead. Sam insisted that Richard wait at the door for Edith and Aubrey while he went to bring the cab. The woman and girl came down just before Sam got back.

Richard asked, "Did you —?"

"Yes, Dick. I was going to throw them away, but I gave them away instead. That way they're gone; he might have wanted to hunt in the rubbish and find them if I'd just thrown —"

"Gave them away? To whom?"

"Funniest thing, Dick. I opened the door and there was an old woman going by in the back hall. Don't know which of the apartments she came from, but she must be a scrub-woman or something, although she looked like a witch really, but when she saw those dolls I had in my hands —"

"Here comes the cab," Dick said. "You gave them to her?"

"Yes, it was funny. She said, 'Mine? To Keep? Forever?' Wasn't that a strange way of asking it? But I laughed and said, 'Yes, ma'am. Yours forev—' "

She broke off, for the shadowy outline of the taxi was at the curb, and Sam opened the door and called out, "Come on, folks!"

Aubrey skipped across the sidewalk into the cab, and the others followed. It started.

The fog was thicker now. They could not see out the windows at all. It was as though a gray wall pressed against the glass, as though the world outside was gone, completely and utterly. Even the windshield, from where they sat, was a gray blank.

"How can he drive so fast?" Richard asked, and there was an edge of nervousness in his voice. "By the way, where are we going, Sam?"

"By George," Sam said, "I forgot to tell her."

"Her?"

"Yeah. Woman driver. They've got them all over now. I'll —"

He leaned forward and tapped on the glass, and the woman turned.

Edith saw her face, and screamed.

THE HAT TRICK

In a sense, the thing never happened. Actually, it would not have happened had not a thundershower been at its height when the four of them came out of the movie.

It had been a horror picture. A really horrible one — not trapdoor claptrap, but a subtle, insidious thing that made the rain-laden night air seem clean and sweet and welcome. To three of them. The fourth —

They stood under the marquee, and Mae said, "Gee, gang, what do we do now, swim or take taxis?" Mae was a cute little blonde with a turned-up nose, the better for smelling the perfumes she sold across a department-store counter.

Elsie turned to the two boys and said, "Let's all go up to my studio for a while. It's early yet." The faint emphasis on the word "studio" was the snapper. Elsie had had the studio for only a week, and the novelty of living in a studio instead of a furnished room made her feel proud and Bohemian and a little wicked. She wouldn't, of course, have invited Walter up alone, but as long as there were two couples of them, it would be all right.

Bob said, "Swell. Listen. Wally, you hold this cab. I'll run down and get some wine. You girls like port?"

Walter and the girls took the cab while Bob talked the bartender, whom he knew slightly, into selling a fifth of wine after legal hours. He came running back with it and they were off to Elsie's.

Mae, in the cab, got to thinking about the horror picture again; she'd almost made them walk out on it. She shivered, and Bob put his arm around her protectively. "Forget it, Mae." he said. "Just a picture. Nothing like that ever happens, really."

"If it did —" Walter began, and then stopped abruptly.

Bob looked at him and said, "If it did, what?"

Walter's voice was a bit apologetic. "Forget now what I was going to say." He smiled, a little strangely, as though the picture had affected him a bit differently than it had affected the others. Quite a bit.

"How's school coming, Walter?" Elsie asked.

Walter was taking a premed course at night school; this was his one night off for the week. Days he worked in a bookstore on Chestnut Street. He nodded and said, "Pretty good."

Elsie was comparing him, mentally, with Mae's boy friend, Bob. Walter wasn't quite as tall as Bob, but he wasn't bad-looking in spite of his glasses. And he was sure a lot smarter than Bob was and would get further some day. Bob was learning printing and was halfway through his apprenticeship now. He'd quit high school in his third year.

When they got to Elsie's studio, she found four glasses in the cupboard, even if they were all different sizes and shapes, and then she rummaged around for crackers and peanut butter while Bob opened the wine and filled the glasses.

It was Elsie's first party in the studio, and it turned out not to be a very wicked one. They talked about the horror picture mostly, and Bob refilled their glasses a couple of times, but none of them felt it much.

Then the conversation ran down a bit and it was still early. Elsie said, "Bob, you used to do some good card tricks. I got a deck in the drawer there. Show us."

That's how it started, as simply as that. Bob took the deck and had Mae draw a card. Then he cut the deck and had Mae put it back in at the cut, and let her cut them a few times, and then he went through the deck, face up, and showed her the card, the nine of spades.

Walter watched without particular interest. He probably wouldn't have said anything if Elsie hadn't piped up, "Bob, that's wonderful. I don't see how you do it." So Walter told her, "It's easy; he looked at the bottom card before he started, and when he cut her card into the deck, that card would be on top of it, so he just picked out the card that was next to it."

Elsie saw the look Bob was giving Walter and she tried to cover up by saying how clever it was even when you knew how it worked, but Bob said, "Wally, maybe you can show us something good. Maybe you're Houdini's pet nephew or something."

Walter grinned at him. He said, "If I had a hat, I might show you one." It was safe; neither of the boys had worn hats. Mae pointed to the tricky little thing she'd taken off her head and put on Elsie's dresser. Walter scowled at it. "Call that a hat? Listen, Bob, I'm sorry I gave your trick away. Skip it; I'm no good at them."

Bob had been riffling the cards back and forth from one hand to the other, and he might have skipped it had not the deck slipped and scattered on the floor. He picked them up and his face was red, not entirely from bending over. He held out the deck to Walter. "You must be good on cards, too," he said. "If you could give my trick away, you must know some. G'wan, do one."

Walter took the deck a little reluctantly, and thought a minute. Then, with Elsie watching him eagerly, he picked out three cards, holding them so no one else could see them, and put the deck back down. Then he held up the three cards, in a V shape, and said, "I'll put one of these on top, one on bottom, and one in the middle of the deck and bring them together with a cut. Look, it's the two of diamonds, the ace of diamonds, and the three of diamonds."

He turned them around again so the backs of the cards were towards his audience and began to place them one on top the deck, one in the middle, and —

"Aw, I get that one," Bob said. "That wasn't the ace of diamonds. It was the ace of hearts and you held it between the other two so just the point of the heart showed. You got that ace of diamonds already planted on top the deck." He grinned triumphantly.

Mae said, "Bob, that was mean. Wally anyway let you finish your stunt before he said anything."

Elsie frowned at Bob, too. Then her face suddenly lit up and she went across to the closet and opened the door and took a cardboard box off the top shelf. "Just remembered this," she said. "It's from a year ago when I had a part in a ballet at the social centre. A top hat."

She opened the box and took it out. It was dented and, despite the box, a bit dusty, but it was indubitably a top hat. She put it, on its crown, on the table near Walter. "You said you could do a good one with a hat, Walter," she said. "Show him."

Everybody was looking at Walter and he shifted uncomfortably. "I — I was just kidding him, Elsie. I don't — I mean it's been so long since I tried that kind of stuff when I was a kid, and everything. I don't remember it."

Bob grinned happily and stood up. His glass and Walter's were empty and he filled them, and he put a little more into the girls' glasses, although they weren't empty yet. Then he picked up a yardstick that was in the corner and flourished it like a circus barker's cane. He said, "Step this way, ladies and gentleman, to see the one and only Walter Beekman do the famous non-existent trick with the black top hat. And in the next cage we have —"

"Bob, shut up," said Mae.

There was a faint glitter in Walter's eyes. He said, "For two cents, I'd —"

Bob reached into his pocket and pulled out a handful of change. He took two pennies out and reached across and dropped them into the inverted top hat. He said, "There you are," and waved the yardstick-cane again. "Price only two cents, the one-fiftieth part of a dollah! Step right up and see the greatest prestidigitatah on earth —"

Walter drank his wine and then his face kept getting redder while Bob went on spieling. Then he stood up. He said quietly, "What'd you like to see for your two cents, Bob?"

Elsie looked at him open-eyed, "You mean, Wally, you're offering to take anything out of —"

"Maybe."

Bob exploded into raucous laughter. He said, "Rats," and reached for the wine bottle.

Walter said, "You asked for it."

He left the top hat right on the table, but he reached out a hand toward it, uncertainly at first. There was a squealing sound from inside the hat, and Walter plunged his hand down in quickly and brought it up holding something by the scruff of the neck.

Mae screamed and then put the back of her hand over her mouth and her eyes were like white saucers. Elsie keeled over quietly on the studio couch in a dead faint; and Bob stood there with his cane-yardstick in midair and his face frozen.

The thing squealed again as Walter lifted it a little higher out of the hat. It looked like a monstrous, hideous black rat. But it was bigger than a rat should be, too big even to have come out of the hat. Its eyes glowed like red light bulbs and it was champing horribly its long scimitar-shaped white teeth, clicking them together with its mouth going several inches open each time and closing like a trap. It wriggled to get the scruff of its neck free of Walter's trembling hand; its clawed forefeet flailed the air. It looked vicious beyond belief.

It squealed incessantly, frightfully, and it smelled with a rank fetid odor as though it had lived in graves and eaten of their contents.

Then, as suddenly as he had pulled his hand out of the hat, Walter pushed it down in again, and the thing down with it. The squealing stopped and Walter took his hand out of the hat. He stood there, shaking, his face pale. He got a handkerchief out of his pocket and mopped sweat off his forehead. His voice sounded strange: "I should never have done it." He ran for the door, opened it, and they heard him stumbling down the stairs.

Mae's hand came away from her mouth slowly and she said, "T-take me home, Bob."

Bob passed a hand across his eyes and said, "Gosh, what —" and went across and looked into the hat. His two pennies were in there, but he didn't reach in to take them out.

He said, his voice cracking once, "What about Elsie? Should we —" Mae got up slowly and said, "Let her sleep it off." They didn't talk much on the way home.

It was two days later that Bob met Elsie on the street. He said, "Hi, Elsie."

And she said, "Hi, there." He said, "Gosh, that was some party we had at your studio the other night. We — we drank too much, I guess."

Something seemed to pass across Elsie's face for a moment, and then she smiled and said, "Well, I sure did; I passed out like a light."

Bob grinned back, and said, "I was a little high myself, I guess. Next time I'll have better manners."

Mae had her next date with Bob the following Monday. It wasn't a double date this time.

After the show, Bob said, "Shall we drop in somewhere for a drink?"

For some reason Mae shivered slightly. "Well, all right, but not wine. I'm off of wine. Say, have you seen Wally since last week?"

Bob shook his head. "Guess you're right about wine. Wally can't take it, either. Made him sick or something and he ran out quick, didn't he? Hope he made the street in time."

Mae dimpled at him. "You weren't so sober yourself, Mr. Evans. Didn't you try to pick a fight with him over some silly card tricks or something? Gee, that picture we saw was awful; I had a nightmare that night."

He smiled. "What about?"

"About a — Gee, I don't remember. Funny how real a dream can be, and still you can't remember just what it was."

Bob didn't see Walter Beekman until one day, three weeks after the party, he dropped into the bookstore. It was a dull hour and Walter, alone in the store, was writing at a desk in the rear. "Hi, Wally. What you doing?"

Walter got up and then nodded toward the papers he'd been working on. "Thesis. This is my last year premed, and I'm majoring in psychology."

Bob leaned negligently against the desk. "Psychology, huh?" he asked tolerantly. "What you writing about?"

Walter looked at him a while before he answered. "Interesting theme. I'm trying to prove that the human mind is incapable of assimilating the utterly incredible. That, in other words, if you saw something you simply couldn't possibly believe, you'd talk yourself out of believing you saw it. You'd rationalize it, somehow."

"You mean if I saw a pink elephant I wouldn't believe it?"

Walter said, "Yes, that or a — Skip it." He went up front to wait on another customer.

When Walter came back, Bob said, "Got a good mystery in the rentals? I got the week-end off; maybe I'll read one."

Walter ran his eye along the rental shelves and then flipped the cover of a book with his forefinger. "Here's a dilly of a weird," he said. "About beings from another world, living here in disguise, pretending they're people."

"What for?"

Walter grinned at him. "Read it and find out. It might surprise you."

Bob moved restlessly and turned to look at the rental books himself. He said, "Aw, I'd rather have a plain mystery story. All that kind of stuff is too much hooey for me." For some reason he didn't quite understand, he looked up at Walter and said, "Isn't it?"

Walter nodded and said, "Yeah, I guess it is."

ARENA

Carson opened his eyes, and found himself looking up-wards into a flickering blue dimness.

It was hot, and he was lying on sand, and a rock embedded in the sand was hurting his back. He rolled over to his side, off the rock, and then pushed himself up to a sitting position.

"I'm crazy," he thought. "Crazy — or dead — or something." The sand was blue, bright blue. And there wasn't any such thing as bright blue sand on Earth or any of the planets. Blue sand under a blue dome that wasn't the sky nor yet a room, but a circumscribed area — somehow he knew it was circumscribed and finite even though he couldn't see to the top of it.

He picked up some of the sand in his hand and let it run through his fingers. It trickled down on to his bare leg. Bare?

He was stark naked, and already his body was dripping perspiration from the enervating heat, coated blue with sand wherever sand had touched it. Elsewhere his body was white.

He thought: then this sand is really blue. If it seemed blue only because of the blue light, then I'd be blue also. But I'm white, so the sand is blue. Blue sand: there isn't any blue sand. There isn't any place like this place I'm in.

Sweat was running down in his eyes. It was hot, hotter than Hell. Only Hell — the Hell of the ancients — was supposed to be red and not blue.

But if this place wasn't Hell, what was it? Only Mercury, among the planets, had heat like this and this wasn't Mercury. And Mercury was some four billion miles from . . . From?

It came back to him then, where he'd been: in the little one-man scouter, outside the orbit of Pluto, scouting a scant million miles to one side of the Earth Armada drawn up in battle array there to intercept the Outsiders.

That sudden strident ringing of the alarm bell when the

rival scouter — the Outsider ship — had come within range of his detectors!

No one knew who the Outsiders were, what they looked like, or from what far galaxy they came, other than that it was in the general direction of the Pleiades.

First, there had been sporadic raids on Earth colonies and outposts; isolated battles between Earth patrols and small groups of Outsider spaceships; battles sometimes won and sometimes lost, but never resulting in the capture of an alien vessel. Nor had any member of a raided colony ever survived to describe the Outsiders who had left the ships, if indeed they had left them.

Not too serious a menace, at first, for the raids had not been numerous or destructive. And individually, the ships had proved slightly inferior in armament to the best of Earth's fighters, although somewhat superior in speed and maneuverability. A sufficient edge in speed, in fact, to give the Outsiders their choice of running or fighting, unless surrounded.

Nevertheless, Earth had prepared for serious trouble, building the mightiest armada of all time. It had been waiting now, that armada, for a long time. Now the showdown was coming.

Scouts twenty billion miles out had detected the approach of a mighty fleet of the Outsiders. Those scouts had never come back, but their radiotronic messages had. And now Earth's armada, all ten thousand ships and half-million fighting spacemen, was out there, outside Pluto's orbit, waiting to intercept and battle to the death.

And an even battle it was going to be, judging by the advance reports of the men of the far picket line who had given their lives to report — before they had died — on the size and strength of the alien fleet.

Anybody's battle, with the mastery of the solar system hanging in the balance, on an even chance. A last and only chance, for Earth and all her colonies lay at the utter mercy of the Outsiders if they ran that gauntlet — Oh yes. Bob Carson remembered now. He remembered that strident bell and his leap for the control panel. His frenzied fumbling as he strapped himself into the seat. The dot in the visiplate that grew larger. The dryness of his mouth. The awful knowledge that this was it for him, at least, although the main fleets were still out of range of one another.

This, his first taste of battle! Within three seconds or less he'd be victorious, or a charred cinder. One hit completely took care of a lightly armed and armoured one-man craft like a scouter.

Frantically — as his lips shaped the word "One" — he worked at the controls to keep that growing dot centred on the crossed spiderwebs of the visiplate. His hands doing that, while his right foot hovered over the pedal that would fire the bolt. The single bolt of concentrated hell that had to hit — or else. There wouldn't be time for any second shot.

"Two." He didn't know he'd said that, either. The dot in the visiplate wasn't a dot now. Only a few thousand miles away, it showed up in the magnification of the plate as though it were only a few hundred yards off. It was a fast little scouter, about the size of his.

An alien ship, all right!

"Thr—" His foot touched the bolt-release pedal.

And then the Outsider had swerved suddenly and was off the crosshairs. Carson punched keys frantically, to follow.

For a tenth of a second, it was out of the visiplate entirely, and then as the nose of his scouter swung after it, he saw it again, diving straight towards the ground.

The ground?

It was an optical illusion of some sort. It had to be: that planet — or whatever it was — that now covered the visiplate couldn't be there. Couldn't possibly! There wasn't any planet nearer than Neptune three billion miles away — with Pluto on the opposite side of the distant pinpoint sun.

His detectors! They hadn't shown any object of planetary dimensions, even of asteroid dimensions, and still didn't.

It couldn't be there, that whatever-it-was he was diving into, only a few hundred miles below him.

In his sudden anxiety to keep from crashing, he forgot the Outsider ship. He fired the front breaking rockets, and even as the sudden change of speed slammed him forward against the seat straps, fired full right for an emergency turn. Pushed them down and held them down, knowing that he needed everything the ship had to keep from crashing and that a turn that sudden would black him out for a moment.

It did black him out.

And that was all. Now he was sitting in hot blue sand, stark naked but otherwise unhurt. No sign of his spaceship and — for that matter — no sign of space. That curve overhead wasn't a sky, whatever else it was.

He scrambled to his feet.

Gravity seemed a little more than Earth-normal. Not much more.

Flat sand stretching away, a few scrawny bushes in clumps here and there. The bushes were blue, too, but in varying shades, some lighter than the blue of the sand, some darker.

Out from under the nearest bush ran a little thing that was like a lizard, except that it had more than four legs. It was blue, too. Bright blue. It saw him and ran back again under the bush.

He looked up again, trying to decide what was overhead. It wasn't exactly a roof, but it was dome-shaped. It flickered and was hard to look at. But definitely, it curved down to the ground, to the blue sand, all around him.

He wasn't far from being under the centre of the dome. At a guess, it was a hundred yards to the nearest wall, if it was a wall. It was as though a blue hemisphere of something about two hundred and fifty yards in circumference was inverted over the flat expanse of the sand.

And everything blue, except one object. Over near a far curving wall there was a red object. Roughly spherical, it seemed to be about a yard in diameter. Too far for him to see clearly through the flickering blueness.

But, unaccountably, he shuddered.

He wiped sweat from his forehead, or tried to, with the back of his hand.

Was this a dream, a nightmare? This heat, this sand, that vague feeling of horror he felt when he looked towards that red thing?

A dream? No, one didn't go to sleep and dream in the midst of a battle in space.

Death? No, never. If there were immortality, it wouldn't be a senseless thing like this, a thing of blue heat and blue sand and a red horror.

Then he heard the voice.

Inside his head he heard it, not with his ears. It came from nowhere or everywhere.

"Through spaces and dimensions wandering," rang the words in his mind, "and in this space and this time, I find two peoples about to exterminate one and so weaken the other that it would retrogress and never fulfill its destiny, but decay and return to mindless dust whence it came. And I say this must not happen."

"Who . . . what are you?" Carson didn't say it aloud, but the question formed itself in his brain.

"You would not understand completely. I am —" There was a pause as though the voice sought — in Carson's brain — for a word that wasn't there, a word he didn't know. "I am the end of evolution of a race so old the time cannot be expressed in words that have meaning to your mind. A race fused into a single entity, eternal.

"An entity such as your primitive race might become" — again the groping for a word — "time from now. So might the race you call, in your mind, the Outsiders. So I intervene in the battle to come, the battle between fleets so evenly matched that destruction of both races will result. One must survive. One must progress and evolve."

"One?" thought Carson. "Mine or —"

"It is in my power to stop the war, to send the Outsiders back to their galaxy. But they would return, or your race would sooner or later follow them there. Only by remaining in this space and time to intervene constantly could I prevent them from destroying one another, and I cannot remain.

"So I shall intervene now. I shall destroy one fleet completely without loss to the other. One civilization shall thus survive."

Nightmare. This had to be nightmare, Carson thought. But he knew it wasn't.

It was too mad, too impossible, to be anything but real.

He didn't dare ask the question — which? But his thoughts asked it for him.

"The stronger shall survive," said the voice. "That I cannot — and would not — change. I merely intervene to make it a complete victory, not" — groping again — "not Pyrrhic victory to a broken race.

"From the outskirts of the not-yet battle I plucked two individuals, you and an Outsider. I see from your mind that, in your early history of nationalisms, battles between champions to decide issues between races were not unknown.

"You and your opponent are here pitted against one another, naked and unarmed, under conditions equally unfamiliar to you both, equally unpleasant to you both. There is no time limit, for here there is no time. The survivor is the champion of his race. That race survives."

"But —" Carson's protest was too inarticulate for expression, but the voice answered it.

"It is fair. The conditions are such that the accident of physical strength will not completely decide the issue. There is a barrier. You will understand. Brain-power and courage will be more important than strength. Most especially courage, which is the will to survive."

"But while this goes on, the fleets will —"

"No, you are in another space, another time. For as long as you are here, time stands still in the universe you know. I see you wonder whether this place is real. It is, and it is not. As I — to your limited understanding — am and am not real. My existence is mental and not physical. You saw me as a planet; it could have been as a dust-mote or a sun.

"But to you this place is now real. What you suffer here will be real. And if you die here, your death will be real. If you die, your failure will be the end of your race. That is enough for you to know."

And then the voice was gone.

Again he was alone, but not alone. For as Carson looked up, he saw that the red thing, the sphere of horror that he now knew was the Outsider, was rolling towards him.

Rolling.

It seemed to have no legs or arms that he could see, no features. It rolled across the sand with the fluid quickness of a drop of mercury. And before it, in some manner he could not understand, came a wave of nauseating hatred.

Carson looked about him frantically. A stone, lying in the sand a few feet away, was the nearest thing to a weapon. It wasn't large, but it had sharp edges, like a slab of flint. It looked a bit like blue flint.

He picked it up, and crouched to receive the attack. It was coming fast, faster than he could run.

No time to think out how he was going to fight it; how anyway could he plan to battle a creature whose strength, whose characteristics, whose method of fighting he did not know? Rolling so fast, it looked more than ever like a perfect sphere.

Ten yards away. Five. And then it stopped.

Rather, it was stopped. Abruptly the near side of it flattened as though it had run up against an invisible wall. It bounced, actually bounced back.

Then it rolled forward again, but more cautiously. It stopped again, at the same place. it tried again, a few yards to one side.

Then it rolled forward again, but more cautiously. It stopped again, at the same place. It tried again, a few yards to one side.

There was a barrier there of some sort. It clicked, then, in

Carson's mind, that thought projected by the Entity who had brought them there:

'— the accident of physical strength will not completely decide the issue. There is a barrier.'

A force-field, of course. Not the Netzian Field, known to Earth science, for that glowed and emitted a crackling sound. This one was invisible, silent.

It was a wall that ran from side to side of the inverted hemisphere; Carson didn't have to verify that himself. The Roller was doing that, rolling sideways along the barrier, seeking a break in it that wasn't there.

Carson took half a dozen steps forward, his left hand groping out before him, and touched the barrier. It felt smooth, yielding, like a sheet of rubber rather than like glass, warm to his touch, but no warmer than the sand underfoot. And it was completely invisible, even at close range.

He dropped the stone and put both hands against it, pushing. It seemed to yield, just a trifle, but no farther than that trifle, even when he pushed with all his weight. It felt like a sheet of rubber backed up by steel. Limited resiliency, and then firm strength.

He stood on tiptoe and reached as high as he could and the barrier was still there.

He saw the Roller coming back, having reached one side of the arena. That feeling of nausea hit Carson again, and he stepped back from the barrier as it went by. It didn't stop.

But did the barrier stop at ground-level? Carson knelt down and burrowed in the sand; it was soft, light, easy to dig in. And two feet down the barrier was still there.

The Roller was coming back again. Obviously, it couldn't find a way through at either side.

There must be a way through, Carson thought, or else this duel is meaningless. —

The Roller was back now, and it stopped just across the barrier, only six feet away. It seemed to be studying him although, for the life of him, Carson couldn't find external evidence of sense organs on the thing. Nothing that looked like eyes or ears, or even a mouth. There was though, he observed, a series of grooves, perhaps a dozen of them altogether, and he saw two tentacles push out from two of the grooves and dip into the sand as though testing its consistency. These were about an inch in diameter and perhaps a foot and a half long.

The tentacles were retractable into the grooves and were kept there except when in use. They retracted when the thing rolled and seemed to have nothing to do with its method of locomotion; that, as far as Carson could judge, seemed to be accomplished by some shifting — just how he couldn't imagine — of its centre of gravity.

He shuddered as he looked at the thing. It was alien, horribly different from anything on Earth or any of the life forms found on the other solar planets. Instinctively, he knew its mind was as alien as its body.

If it could project that almost tangible wave of hatred, perhaps it could read his mind as well, sufficiently for his purpose.

Deliberately, Carson picked up the rock that had been his only weapon, then tossed it down again in a gesture of relinquishment and raised his empty hands, palms up, before him.

He spoke aloud, knowing that although the words would be meaningless to the creature before him, speaking them would focus his own thoughts more completely upon the message.

"Can we not have peace between us?" he said, his voice strange in the stillness. "The Entity who brought us here has told us what must happen if our races fight — extinction of one and weakening and retrogression of the other. The battle between them, said the Entity, depends upon what we do here. Why cannot we agree to an eternal peace — your race to its galaxy, we to ours?"

Carson blanked out his mind to receive a reply.

It came, and it staggered him back, physically. He recoiled several steps in sheer horror at the intensity of the lust-to-kill of the red images projected at him. For a moment that seemed eternity he had to struggle against the impact of that hatred, fighting to clear his mind of it and drive out the alien thoughts to which he had given admittance. He wanted to retch.

His mind cleared slowly. He was breathing hard and he felt weaker, but he could think.

He stood studying the Roller. It had been motionless during the mental duel it had so nearly won. Now it rolled a few feet to one side, to the nearest of the blue bushes. Three tentacles whipped out of their grooves and began to investigate the bush.

"O.K.," Carson said, "so it's war then." He managed a grin. "If I got your answer straight, peace doesn't appeal to you." And, because he was, after all, a young man and couldn't resist the impulse to be dramatic, he added, "To the death!"

But his voice, in that utter silence, sounded silly even to himself. It came to him, then, that this was to the death, not only his own death or that of the red spherical thing which he thought of as the Roller, but death to the entire race of one or the other of them: the end of the human race, if he failed.

It made him suddenly very humble and very afraid to think that. With a knowledge that was above even faith, he knew that the Entity who had arranged this duel had told the truth about its intentions and its powers. The future of humanity depended upon him. It was an awful thing to realize. He had to concentrate on the situation at hand.

There had to be some way of getting through the barrier, or of killing through the barrier.

Mentally? He hoped that wasn't all, for the Roller obviously had stronger telepathic powers than the undeveloped ones of the human race. Or did it?

He had been able to drive the thoughts of the Roller out of his own mind; could it drive out his? If its ability to project were stronger, might not its receptivity mechanism be more vulnerable?

He stared at it and endeavoured to concentrate and focus all his thought upon it.

"Die," he thought. "You are going to die. You are dying. You are —"

He tried variations on it, and mental pictures. Sweat stood out on his forehead and he found himself trembling with the intensity of the effort. But the Roller went ahead with its investigation of the bush, as utterly unaffected as though Carson had been reciting the multiplication table.

So that was no good.

He felt dizzy from the heat and his strenuous effort at concentration. He sat down on the blue sand and gave his full attention to studying the Roller. By study, perhaps, he could judge its strength and detect its weaknesses, learn things that would be valuable to know when and if they should come to grips.

It was breaking off twigs. Carson watched carefully, trying to judge just how hard it worked to do that. Later, he thought, he could find a similar bush on his own side, break off twigs of equal thickness himself, and gain a comparison of physical strength between his own arms and hands and those tentacles.

The twigs broke off hard; the Roller was having to struggle with each one. Each tentacle, he saw, bifurcated at the tip into two fingers, each tipped by a nail or claw. The claws didn't seem to be particularly long or dangerous, or no more so than his own fingernails, if they were left to grow a bit.

No, on the whole, it didn't look too hard to handle physically. Unless, of course, that bush was made of pretty tough stuff. Carson looked round; within reach was another bush of identically the same type.

He snapped off a twig. It was brittle, easy to break. Of course, the Roller might have been faking deliberately but he didn't think so. On the other hand, where was it vulnerable? How would he go about killing it if he got the chance? He went back to studying it. The outer hide looked pretty tough; he'd need a sharp weapon of some sort. He picked up the piece of rock again. It was about twelve inches long, narrow, and fairly sharp on one end. If it chipped like flint, he could make a serviceable knife out of it.

The Roller was continuing its investigations of the bushes. It rolled again, to the nearest one of another type. A little blue lizard, many-legged like the one Carson had seen on his side of the barrier, darted out from under the bush.

A tentacle of the Roller lashed out and caught it, picked it up. Another tentacle whipped over and began to pull legs off the lizard, as coldly as it had pulled twigs off the bush. The creature struggled frantically and emitted a shrill squealing that was the first sound Carson had heard here, other than the sound of his own voice.

Carson made himself continue to watch; anything he could learn about his opponent might prove valuable, even knowledge of its unnecessary cruelty — particularly, he thought with sudden emotion, knowledge of its unnecessary cruelty. It would make it a pleasure to kill the thing, if and when the chance came.

With half its legs gone, the lizard stopped squealing and lay limp in the Roller's grasp.

It didn't continue with the rest of the legs. Contemptuously it tossed the dead lizard away from it, in Carson's direction. The lizard arced through the air between them and landed at his feet.

It had come through the barrier! The barrier wasn't there any more! Carson was on his feet in a flash, the knife gripped tightly in his hand, leaping forward. He'd settle this thing here and now! With the barrier gone — but it wasn't gone. He found that out the hard way, running head on into it and nearly knocking himself silly. He bounced back and fell.

As he sat up, shaking his head to clear it, he saw something coming through the air towards him, and threw himself flat again on the sand, to one side. He got his body out of the way, but there was a sudden sharp pain in the calf of his left leg.

He rolled backwards, ignoring the pain, and scrambled to

his feet. It was a rock, he saw now, that had struck him. And the Roller was picking up another, swinging it back gripped between two tentacles, ready to throw again.

It sailed through the air towards him, but he was able to step out of its way. The Roller, apparently, could throw straight, but neither hard nor far. The first rock had struck him only because he had been sitting down and had not seen it coming until it was almost upon him.

Even as he stepped aside from that weak second throw Carson drew back his right arm and let fly with the rock that was still in his hand. If missiles, he thought with elation, can cross the barrier, then two can play at the game of throwing them.

He couldn't miss a three-foot sphere at only four-yard range, and he didn't miss. The rock whizzed straight, and with a speed several times that of the missiles the Roller had thrown. It hit dead centre, but hit flat instead of point first. But it hit with a resounding thump, and obviously hurt. The Roller had been reaching for another rock, but changed its mind and got out of there instead. By the time Carson could pick up and throw another rock, the Roller was forty yards back from the barrier and going strong.

His second throw missed by feet, and his third throw was short. The Roller was out of range of any missile heavy enough to be damaging.

Carson grinned. That round had been his.

He stopped grinning as he bent over to examine the calf of his leg. A jagged edge of the stone had made a cut several inches long. It was bleeding pretty freely, but he didn't think it had gone deep enough to hit an artery. If it stopped bleeding of its own accord, well and good. If not, he was in for trouble.

Finding out one thing, though, took precedence over that cut: the nature of the barrier.

He went forward to it again, this time groping with his hands before him. Holding one hand against it, he tossed a handful of sand at it with the other hand. The sand went right through; his hand didn't.

Organic matter versus inorganic? No, because the dead lizard had gone through it, and a lizard, alive or dead, was certainly organic. Plant life? He broke off a twig and poked it at the barrier. The twig went through, with no resistance, but when his fingers gripping the twig came to the barrier, they were stopped.

He couldn't get through it, nor could the Roller. But rocks and sand and a dead lizard. . . . How about a live lizard?

He went hunting under bushes until he found one, and caught it. He tossed it against the barrier and it bounced back and scurried away across the blue sand.

That gave him the answer, so far as he could determine it now. The screen was a barrier to living things. Dead or inorganic matter could cross it.

With that off his mind, Carson looked at his injured leg again. The bleeding was lessening, which meant he wouldn't need to worry about making a tourniquet. But he should find some water, if any was available, to clean the wound.

Water — the thought of it made him realize that he was getting awfully thirsty. He'd have to find water, in case this contest turned out to be a protracted one.

Limping slightly now, he started off to make a circuit of his half of the arena. Guiding himself with one hand along the barrier, he walked to his right until he came to the curving sidewall. It was visible, a dull blue-grey at close range, and the surface of it felt just like the central barrier.

He experimented by tossing a handful of sand at it, and the sand reached the wall and disappeared as it went through. The hemispherical shell was a force-field, too, but an opaque one, instead of transparent like the barrier.

He followed it round until he came back to the barrier, and walked back along the barrier to the point from which he'd started.

No sign of water.

Worried now, he started a series of zigzags back and forth between the barrier and the wall, covering the intervening space thoroughly.

No water. Blue sand, blue bushes, and intolerable heat. Nothing else.

It must be his imagination, he told himself that he was suffering that much from thirst. How long had he been there? Of course, no time at all, according to his own space-time frame. The Entity had told him time stood still out there, while he was here. But his body processes went on here, just the same. According to his body's reckoning, how long had he been here? Three or four hours, perhaps. Certainly not long enough to be suffering from thirst.

Yet he was suffering from it; his throat was dry and parched. Probably the intense heat was the cause. It was hot, a hundred and thirty Fahrenheit, at a guess. A dry, still heat without the slightest movement of air.

He was limping rather badly and utterly fagged when he finished the futile exploration of his domain.

He stared across at the motionless Roller and hoped it was as miserable as he was. The Entity had said the conditions here were equally unfamiliar and uncomfortable for both of them. Maybe the Roller came from a planet where two-hundred-degree heat was the norm; maybe it was freezing while he was roasting. Maybe the air was as much too thick for it as it was too thin for him. For the exertion of his explorations had left him panting. The atmosphere here, he realized, was not much thicker than on Mars.

No water. That meant a deadline, for him at any rate. Unless he could find a way to cross that barrier or to kill his enemy from this side of it, thirst would kill him eventually.

It gave him a feeling of desperate urgency, but he made himself sit down a moment to rest, to think.

What was there to do? Nothing, and yet so many things. The several varieties of bushes, for example; they didn't look promising, but he'd have to examine them for possibilities. And his leg — he'd have to do something about that, even without water to clean it; gather ammunition in the form of rocks; find a rock that would make a good knife.

His leg hurt rather badly now, and he decided that came

first. One type of bush had leaves — or things rather similar to leaves. He pulled off a handful of them and decided, after examination, to take a chance on them. He used them to clean off the sand and dirt and caked blood, then made a pad of fresh leaves and tied it over the wound with tendrils from the same bush.

The tendrils proved unexpectedly tough and strong.

They were slender and pliable, yet he couldn't break them at all, and had to saw them off the bush with the sharp edge of blue flint. Some of the thicker ones were over a foot long, and he filed away in his memory, for future reference, the fact that a bunch of the thick ones, tied together, would make a pretty serviceable rope. Maybe he'd be able to think of a use for rope.

Next, he made himself a knife. The blue flint did chip. From a foot-long splinter of it, he fashioned himself a crude but lethal weapon. And of tendrils from the bush, he made himself a rope-belt through which he could thrust the flint knife, to keep it with him all the time and yet have his hands free.

He went back to studying the bushes. There were three other types. One was leafless, dry, brittle, rather like a dried tumbleweed. Another was of soft, crumbly wood, almost like punk. It looked and felt as though it would make excellent tinder for a fire. The third type was the most nearly woodlike. It had fragile leaves that wilted at the touch, but the stalks, although short, were straight and strong.

It was horribly, unbearably hot.

He limped up to the barrier, felt to make sure that it was still there. It was. He stood watching the Roller for a while; it was keeping a safe distance from the barrier, out of effective stone-throwing range. It was moving around back there, doing something. He couldn't tell what it was doing.

Once it stopped moving, came a little closer, and seemed to concentrate its attention on him. Again Carson had to fight off a wave of nausea. He threw a stone at it; the Roller retreated and went back to whatever it had been doing before.

At least he could make it keep its distance. And, he thought bitterly, a lot of good that did him. Just the same, he spent the next hour or two gathering stones of suitable size for throwing, and making several piles of them near his side of the barrier.

His throat burned now. It was difficult for him to think about anything except water. But he had to think about other things: about getting through that barrier, under or over it, getting at that red sphere and killing it before this place of heat and thirst killed him.

The barrier went to the wall upon either side, but how high, and how far under the sand?

For a moment, Carson's mind was too fuzzy to think out how he could find out either of those things. Idly, sitting there in the hot sand — and he didn't remember sitting down — he watched a blue lizard crawl from the shelter of one bush to the shelter of another.

From under the second bush, it looked out at him.

Carson grinned at it, recalling the old story of the desert-colonists on Mars, taken from an older story of Earth — "Pretty soon you get so lonesome you find yourself talking to the lizards, and then not so long after that you find the lizards talking back to you. . . ."

He should have been concentrating, of course, on how to kill the Roller, but instead he grinned at the lizard and said, "Hello, there."

The lizard took a few steps towards him. "Hello," it said.

Carson was stunned for a moment, and then he put back his head and roared with laughter. It didn't hurt his throat to do so, either; he hadn't been that thirsty.

Why not? Why should the Entity who thought up this nightmare of a place not have a sense of humour, along with the other powers he had? Talking lizards, equipped to talk back in my own language, if I talk to them — it's a nice touch.

He grinned at the lizard and said, "Come on over." But the lizard turned and ran away, scurrying from bush to bush until it was out of sight.

He had to get past the barrier. He couldn't get through it, or over it, but was he certain he couldn't get under it? And come to think of it, didn't one sometimes find water by digging?

Painfully now, Carson limped up to the barrier and started digging, scooping up sand a double handful at a time. It was slow work because the sand ran in at the edges and the deeper he got the bigger in diameter the hole had to be. How many hours it took him, he didn't know, but he hit bedrock four feet down: dry bedrock with no sign of water.

The force-field of the barrier went down clear to the bedrock.

He crawled out of the hole and lay there panting, then raised his head to look across and see what the Roller was doing.

It was making something out of wood from the bushes, tied together with tendrils, a queerly shaped framework about four feet high and roughly square. To see it better, Carson climbed on to the mound of sand he had excavated and stood there staring.

There were two long levers sticking out of the back of it, one with a cup-shaped affair on the end. Seemed to be some sort of a catapult, Carson thought.

Sure enough, the Roller was lifting a sizable rock into the cup-shape. One of his tentacles moved the other lever up and down for a while, and then he turned the machine slightly, aiming it, and the lever with the stone flew up and forward.

The stone curved several yards over Carson's head, so far away that he didn't have to duck, but he judged the distance it had travelled, and whistled softly. He couldn't throw a rock that weight more than half that distance. And even retreating to the rear of his domain wouldn't put him out of range of that machine if the Roller pushed it forward to the barrier.

Another rock whizzed over, not quite so far away this time.

Moving from side to side along the barrier, so the catapult couldn't bracket him, he hurled a dozen rocks at it. But that wasn't going to be any good, he saw. They had to be light rocks, or he couldn't throw them that far. If they hit the framework, they bounced off harmlessly. The Roller had no difficulty, at that distance, in moving aside from those that came near it.

Besides, his arm was tiring badly. He ached all over.

He stumbled to the rear of the arena. Even that wasn't any good; the rocks reached back there, too, only there were longer intervals between them, as though it took longer to wind up the mechanism, whatever it was, of the catapult.

Wearily he dragged himself back to the barrier again. Several times he fell and could barely rise to his feet to go on. He was, he knew, near the limit of his endurance. Yet he didn't dare stop moving now, until and unless he could put that catapult out of action. If he fell asleep, he'd never wake up.

One of the stones from it gave him the glimmer of an idea. It hit one of the piles of stones he'd gathered near the barrier to use as ammunition and struck sparks.

Sparks! Fire! Primitive man had made fire by striking sparks, and with some of those dry crumbly bushes as tinder . . .

A bush of that type grew near him. He uprooted it, took it over to the pile of stones, then patiently hit one stone against another until a spark touched the punklike wood of the bush. It went up in flames so fast that it singed his eyebrows and was burned to an ash within seconds.

But he had the idea now, and within minutes had a little fire going in the lee of the mound of sand he'd made. The tinder bushes started it, and other bushes which burned more slowly kept it a steady flame.

The tough tendrils didn't burn readily; that made the firebombs easy to rig and throw; a bundle of faggots tied about a small stone to give it weight and a loop of the tendril to swing it by.

He made half a dozen of them before he lighted and threw the first. It went wide, and the Roller started a quick retreat, pulling the catapult after him. But Carson had the others ready and threw them in rapid succession. The fourth wedged in the catapult's framework and did the trick. The Roller tried desperately to put out the spreading blaze by throwing sand, but its clawed tentacles would take only a spoonful at a time and its efforts were ineffectual. The catapult burned.

The Roller moved safely away from the fire and seemed to concentrate its attention on Carson. Again he felt that wave of hatred and nausea — but more weakly; either the Roller itself was weakening or Carson had learned how to protect himself against the mental attack.

He thumbed his nose at it and then sent it scuttling back to safety with a stone. The Roller went to the back of its half of the arena and started pulling up bushes again. Probably it was going to make another catapult.

Carson verified that the barrier was still operating, and then found himself sitting in the sand beside it, suddenly too weak to stand up.

His leg throbbed steadily now and the pangs of thirst were severe. But those things paled beside the physical exhaustion that gripped his entire body.

Hell must be like this, he thought, the Hell that the ancients had believed in. He fought to stay awake, and yet staying awake seemed futile, for there was nothing he could do while the barrier remained impregnable and the Roller stayed back out of range.

He tried to remember what he had read in books of archaeology about the methods of fighting used back in the days before metal and plastic. The stone missile had come first, he thought. Well, that he already had.

Bow and arrow? No; he'd tried archery once and knew his own ineptness even with a modern sportsman's dura-steel weapon, made for accuracy. With only the crude, pieced-together outfit he could make here, he doubted if he could shoot as far as he could throw a rock.

Spear? Well, he could make that. It would be useless at any distance, but would be a handy thing at close range, if he ever got to close range. Making one would help keep his mind from wandering, as it was beginning to do.

He was still beside one of the piles of stones. He sorted through it until he found one shaped roughly like a spearhead. With a smaller stone he began to chip it into shape, fashioning sharp shoulders on the sides so that if it penetrated it would not pull out again like a harpoon. A harpoon was better than a spear, maybe, for this crazy contest. If he could once get it into the Roller, and had a rope on it, he could pull the Roller up against the barrier and the stone blade of his knife would reach through that barrier, even if his hands wouldn't.

The shaft was harder to make than the head, but by splitting and joining the main stems of four of the bushes, and wrapping the joints with the tough but thin tendrils, he got a strong shaft about four feet long, and tied the stone head in a notch cut in one end. It was crude, but strong.

With the tendrils he made himself twenty feet of line. It was light and didn't look strong, but he knew it would hold his weight and to spare. He tied one end of it to the shaft of the harpoon and the other end about his right wrist. At least, if he threw his harpoon across the barrier, he'd be able to pull it back if he missed.

He tried to stand up, to see what the Roller was doing, and found he couldn't get to his feet. On the third try, he got as far as his knees and then fell flat again.

"I've got to sleep," he thought. "If a showdown came now, I'd be helpless. He could come up here and kill me, if he knew. I've got to regain some strength."

Slowly, painfully, he crawled back from the barrier.

The jar of something thudding against the sand near him wakened him from a confused and horrible dream to a more confused and horrible reality, and he opened his eyes again to blue radiance over blue sand.

How long had he slept? A minute? A day?

Another stone thudded nearer and threw sand on him. He got his arms under him and sat up. He turned round and saw the Roller twenty yards away, at the barrier.

It rolled off hastily as he sat up, not stopping until it was as far away as it could get.

He'd fallen asleep too soon, he realized, while he was still in range of the Roller's throwing. Seeing him lying motionless, it had dared come up to the barrier. Luckily, it didn't realize how weak he was, or it could have stayed there and kept on throwing stones.

He started crawling again, this time forcing himself to keep going until he was as far as he could go, until the opaque wall of the arena's outer shell was only a yard away.

Then things slipped away again. . . .

When he awoke, nothing about him was changed, but this time he knew that he had slept a long while. The first thing he became aware of was the inside of his mouth; it was dry, caked. His tongue was swollen.

Something was wrong, he knew, as he returned slowly to full awareness. He felt less tired, the stage of utter exhaustion had passed. But there was pain, agonizing pain. It wasn't until he tried to move that he knew that it came from his leg.

He raised his head and looked down at it. It was swollen below the knee, and the swelling showed even half-way up his thigh. The plant tendrils he had tied round the protective pad of leaves now cut deeply into his flesh.

To get his knife under that embedded lashing would have been impossible. Fortunately, the final knot was over the shin bone where the vine cut in less deeply than elsewhere. He was able, after an effort, to untie the knot.

A look under the pad of leaves showed him the worst: infection and blood poisoning. Without drugs, without even water, there wasn't a thing he could do about it, except die when the poison spread through his system.

He knew it was hopeless, then, and that he'd lost, and with him, humanity. When he died here, out there in the universe he knew, all his friends, everybody, would die too. Earth and the colonized planets would become the home of the red, rolling, alien Outsiders.

It was that thought which gave him courage to start crawling, almost blindly, towards the barrier again, pulling himself along by his arms and hands.

There was a chance in a million that he'd have strength left when he got there to throw his harpoon-spear just once, and with deadly effect, if the Roller would come up to the barrier, or if the barrier was gone.

It took him years, it seemed, to get there. The barrier wasn't gone. It was as impassable as when he'd first felt it.

The Roller wasn't at the barrier. By raising himself up on his elbows, he could see it at the back of its part of the arena, working on a wooden framework that was a half-completed duplicate of the catapult he'd destroyed.

It was moving slowly now. Undoubtedly it had weakened, too.

Carson doubted that it would ever need that second catapult. He'd be dead, he thought, before it was finished.

His mind must have slipped for a moment, for he found himself beating his fists against the barrier in futile rage, and made himself stop. He closed his eyes, tried to make himself calm.

"Hello," said a voice.

It was a small, thin voice. He opened his eyes and turned his head. It was a lizard.

"Go away," Carson wanted to say. "Go away; you're not really there, or you're there but not really talking. I'm imagining things again."

But he couldn't talk; his throat and tongue were past all speech with the dryness. He closed his eyes again.

"Hurt," said the voice. "Kill. Hurt — kill. Come."

He opened his eyes again. The blue ten-legged lizard was still there. It ran a little way along the barrier, came back, started off again, and came back.

"Hurt," it said. "Kill. Come."

Again it started off, and came back. Obviously it wanted Carson to follow it along the barrier.

He closed his eyes again. The voice kept on. The same

three meaningless words. Each time he opened his eyes, it ran off and came back.

"Hurt. Kill. Come."

Carson groaned. Since there would be no peace unless he followed the thing, he crawled after it.

Another sound, a high-pitched, squealing, came to his ears. There was something lying in the sand, writhing, squealing. Something small, blue, that looked like a lizard.

He saw it was the lizard whose legs the Roller had pulled off, so long ago. It wasn't dead; it had come back to life and was wriggling and screaming in agony.

"Hurt," said the other lizard. "Hurt. Kill. Kill."

Carson understood. He took the flint knife from his belt and killed the tortured creature. The live lizard scurried off.

Carson turned back to the barrier. He leaned his hands and head against it and watched the Roller, far back, working on the new catapult.

"I could get that far," he thought, "if I could get through. If I could get through, I might win yet. It looks weak, too. I might —"

And then there was another reaction of hopelessness, when pain sapped his will and he wished that he were dead, envying the lizard he'd just killed. It didn't have to live on and suffer.

He was pushing on the barrier with the flat of his hands when he noticed his arms, how thin and scrawny they were. He must really have been here a long time, for days, to get as thin as that.

For a while he was almost hysterical again, and then came a time of deep calm and thought.

The lizard he had just killed had crossed the barrier, still alive. It had come from the Roller's side; the Roller had pulled off its legs and then tossed it contemptuously at him and it had come through the barrier.

It hadn't been dead, merely unconscious. A live lizard couldn't go through the barrier, but an unconscious one could. The barrier was not a barrier, then, to living flesh, but to conscious flesh. It was a mental protection, a mental hazard.

With that thought, Carson started crawling along the barrier to make his last desperate gamble, a hope so forlorn that only a dying man would have dared try it.

He moved along the barrier to the mound of sand, about four feet high, which he'd scooped out while trying — how many days ago? — to dig under the barrier or to reach water. That mound lay right at the barrier, its farther slope half on one side of the barrier, half on the other.

Taking with him a rock from the pile nearby, he climbed up to the top of the dune and lay there against the barrier, so that if the barrier were taken away he'd roll on down the short slope, into the enemy territory.

He checked to be sure that the knife was safely in his rope belt, that the harpoon was in the crook of his left arm and that the twenty-foot rope fastened to it and to his wrist. Then with his right hand he raised the rock with which he would hit himself on the head. Luck would have to be with him on that blow; it would have to be hard enough to knock him out, but not hard enough to knock him out for long.

He had a hunch that the Roller was watching him, and would see him roll down through the barrier, and come to investigate. It would believe he was dead, he hoped — he thought it had probably drawn the same deduction about the nature of the barrier that he had. But it would come cautiously; he would have a little time — He struck himself.

Pain brought him back to consciousness, a sudden, sharp pain in his hip that was different from the pain in his head and leg. He had, thinking things out before he had struck himself, anticipated that very pain, even hoped for it, and had steeled himself against awakening with a sudden movement.

He opened his eyes just a slit, and saw that he had guessed rightly. The Roller was coming closer. It was twenty feet away; the pain that had awakened him was the stone it had tossed to see whether he was alive or dead. He lay still. It came closer, fifteen feet away, and stopped again. Carson scarcely breathed.

As nearly as possible, he was keeping his mind a blank, lest its telepathic ability detect consciousness in him. And with his mind blanked out that way, the impact of its thoughts upon his mind was shattering.

He felt sheer horror at the alienness, the differentness of those thoughts, conveying things that he felt but could not understand or express, because no terrestrial language had words, no terrestrial brain had images to fit them. The mind of a spider, he thought, or the mind of a praying mantis or a Martian sand-serpent, raised to intelligence and put in telepathic rapport with human minds, would be a homely familiar thing, compared to this.

He understood now that the Entity had been right: Man or Roller, the universe was not a place that could hold them both.

Closer. Carson waited until it was only feet away, until its clawed tentacles reached out. . . .

Oblivious to agony now, he sat up, raised and flung the harpoon with all the strength that remained to him. As the Roller, deeply stabbed by the harpoon, rolled away, Carson tried to get to his feet to run after it. He couldn't do that; he fell, but kept crawling.

It reached the end of the rope, and he was jerked forward by the pull on his wrist. It dragged him a few feet and then stopped. Carson kept going, pulling himself towards it hand over hand along the rope. It stopped there, tentacles trying in vain to pull out the harpoon. It seemed to shudder and quiver, and then realized that it couldn't get away, for it rolled back towards him, clawed tentacles reaching out.

Stone knife in hand, he met it. He stabbed, again and again, while those horrid claws ripped skin and flesh and muscle from his body.

He stabbed and slashed, and at last it was still.

A bell was ringing, and it took him a while after he'd opened his eyes to tell where he was and what it was. He was strapped into the seat of his scouter, and the visiplate before him showed only empty space. No Outsider ship and no impossible planet.

The bell was the communications plate signal; someone wanted him to switch power into the receiver. Purely reflex action enabled him to reach forward and throw the lever.

The face of Brander, captain of the Magellan, mothership of his group of scouters, flashed into the screen. His face was pale and his black eyes glowing with excitement.

"Magellan to Carson," he snapped. "Come on in. The fight's over. We've won!"

The screen went blank; Brander would be signaling the other scouters of his command.

Slowly, Carson set the controls for the return. Slowly, unbelievingly, he unstrapped himself from the seat and went back to get a drink at the cold water tank. For some reason, he was unbelievably thirsty. He drank six glasses.

He leaned there against the wall, trying to think.

Had it happened? He was in good health, sound, uninjured. His thirst had been mental rather than physical; his throat hadn't been dry.

He pulled up his trouser leg and looked at the calf. There was a long white scar there, but a perfectly healed scar; it hadn't been there before. He zipped open the front of his shirt and saw that his chest and abdomen were criss-crossed with tiny, almost unnoticeable, perfectly healed scars.

It had happened!

The scouter, under automatic control, was already entering the hatch of the mother-ship. The grapples pulled it into its individual lock, and a moment later a buzzer indicated that the lock was airfilled. Carson opened the hatch and stepped outside, went through the double door of the lock.

He went right to Brander's office, went in, and saluted.

Brander still looked dazed. "Hi, Carson," he said. "What you missed; what a show!"

"What happened, sir?"

"Don't know, exactly. We fired one salvo, and their whole

fleet went up in dust! Whatever it was jumped from ship to ship in a flash, even the ones we hadn't aimed at and that were out of range! The whole fleet disintegrated before our eyes, and we didn't get the paint of a single ship scratched!

"We can't even claim credit for it. Must have been some unstable component in the metal they used, and our sighting shot just set it off. Man, too bad you missed all the excitement!"

Carson managed a sickly ghost of a grin, for it would be days before he'd be over the impact of his experience, but the captain wasn't watching.

"Yes, sir," he said. Common sense, more than modesty, told him he'd be branded as the worst liar in space if he ever said any more than that. "Yes, sir, too bad I missed all the excitement. . . ."

DON'T LOOK BEHIND YOU

Just sit back and relax, now. Try to enjoy this; it's going be the last story you ever read, or nearly the last. After you finish it you can sit there and stall a while, you can find excuses to hang around your house, or your room, or your office, wherever you're reading this; but sooner or later you're going to have to get up and go out. That's where I'm waiting for you: outside. Or maybe closer than that. Maybe in this room.

You think that's a joke of course. You think this is just a story in a book, and that I don't really mean you. Keep right on thinking so. But be fair; admit that I'm giving you fair warning.

Harley bet me I couldn't do it. He bet me a diamond he's told me about, a diamond as big as his head. So you see why I've got to kill you. And why I've got to tell you how and why and all about it first. That's part of the bet. It's just the kind of idea Harley would have.

I'll tell you about Harley first. He's tall and handsome, and suave and cosmopolitan. He looks something like Ronald Coleman, only he's taller. He dresses like a million dollars, but it wouldn't matter if he didn't; I mean that he'd look distinguished in overalls. There's a sort of magic about Harley, a mocking magic in the way he looks at you; it makes you think of palaces and far-off countries and bright music.

It was in Springfield, Ohio, that he met Justin Dean. Justin was a funny-looking little runt who was just a printer. He worked for the Atlas Printing & Engraving Company. He was a very ordinary little guy, just about as different as possible from Harley; you couldn't pick two men more different. He was only thirty-five, but he was mostly bald already, and he had to wear thick glasses because he'd worn out his eyes doing fine printing and engraving. He was a good printer and engraver; I'll say that for him.

I never asked Harley how he happened to come to Springfield, but the day he got there, after he'd checked in at the Castle Hotel, he stopped in at Atlas to have some calling cards made. It happened that Justin Dean was alone in the shop at the time, and he took Harley's order for the cards; Harley wanted engraved ones, the best. Harley always wants the best of everything.

Harley probably didn't even notice Justin; there was no reason why he should have. But Justin noticed Harley all right, and in him he saw everything that he himself would like to be, and never would be, because most of the things Harley has, you have to be born with.

And Justin made the plates for the cards himself and printed them himself, and he did a wonderful job — something he thought would be worthy of a man like Harley Prentice. That was the name engraved on the card, just that and nothing else, as all really important people have their cards engraved.

He did fine-line work on it, freehand cursive style, and used all the skill he had. It wasn't wasted, because the next day when Harley called to get the cards he held one and stared at it for a while, and then he looked at Justin, seeing him for the first time. He asked, "Who did this?"

And little Justin told him proudly who had done it, and Harley smiled at him and told him it was the work of an artist, and he asked Justin to have dinner with him that evening after work, in the Blue Room of the Castle Hotel.

That's how Harley and Justin got together, but Harley was careful. He waited until he'd known Justin a while before he asked him whether or not he could make plates for five and ten dollar bills. Harley had the contacts; he could market the bills in quantity with men who specialized in passing them, and — most important — he knew where he could get paper with the silk threads in it, paper that wasn't quite the genuine thing, but was close enough to pass inspection by anyone but an expert.

So Justin quit his job at Atlas and he and Harley went to

New York, and they set up a little printing shop as a blind, on Amsterdam Avenue south of Sherman Square, and they worked at the bills. Justin worked hard, harder than he had ever worked in his life, because besides working on the plates for the bills, he helped meet expenses by handling what legitimate printing work came into the shop.

He worked day and night for almost a year, making plate after plate, and each one was a little better than the last, and finally he had plates that Harley said were good enough. That night they had dinner at the Waldorf-Astoria to celebrate and after dinner they went the rounds of the best night clubs, and it cost Harley a small fortune, but that didn't matter because they were going to get rich.

They drank champagne, and it was the first time Justin ever drank champagne, and he got disgustingly drunk and must have made quite a fool of himself. Harley told him about it afterwards, but Harley wasn't mad at him. He took him back to his room at the hotel and put him to bed, and Justin was pretty sick for a couple of days. But that didn't matter, either, because they were going to get rich.

Then Justin started printing bills from the plates, and they got rich. After that, Justin didn't have to work so hard, either, because he turned down most jobs that came into the print shop, told them he was behind schedule and couldn't handle any more. He took just a little work, to keep up a front. And behind the front, he made five and ten dollar bills, and he and Harley got rich.

He got to know other people whom Harley knew. He met Bull Mallon, who handled the distribution end. Bull Mallon was built like a bull; that was why they called him that. He had a face that never smiled or changed expression at all except when he was holding burning matches to the soles of Justin's bare feet. But that wasn't then; that was later, when he wanted Justin to tell him where the plates were.

And he got to know Captain John Willys of the Police Department, who was a friend of Harley's, to whom Harley gave quite a bit of the money they made, but that didn't matter either, because there was plenty left and they all got rich. He met a friend of Harley's who was a big star of the stage, and one who owned a big New York newspaper. He got to know other people equally important, but in less respectable ways.

Harley, Justin knew, had a hand in lots of other enterprises besides the little mint on Amsterdam Avenue. Some of these ventures took him out of town, usually over weekends. And the weekend that Harley was murdered Justin never found out what really happened, except that Harley went away and didn't come back. Oh, he knew that he was murdered, all right, because the police found his body — with three bullet holes in his chest — in the most expensive suite of the best hotel in Albany. Even for a place to be found dead in Harley Prentice had chosen the best.

All Justin ever knew about it was that a long distance call came to him at the hotel where he was staying, the night that Harley was murdered — it must have been a matter of minutes, in fact, before the time the newspapers said Harley was killed.

It was Harley's voice on the phone, and his voice was debonair and unexcited as ever. But he said, "Justin? Get to the shop and get rid of the plates, the paper, everything. Right away. I'll explain when I see you." He waited only until Justin said, "Sure, Harley," and then he said, "Attaboy," and hung up.

Justin hurried around to the printing shop and got the plates and the paper and a few thousand dollars' worth of counterfeit bills that were on hand. He made the paper and bills into one bundle and the copper plates into another, smaller one, and he left the shop with no evidence that it had ever been a mint in miniature.

He was very careful and very clever in disposing of both bundles. He got rid of the big one first by checking in at a big hotel, not one he or Harley ever stayed at, under a false name, just to have a chance to put the big bundle in the incinerator there. It was paper and it would burn. And he made sure there was a fire in the incinerator before he dropped it down the chute.

The plates were different. They wouldn't burn, he knew, so he took a trip to Staten Island and back on the ferry and, somewhere out in the middle of the bay, he dropped the bundle over the side into the water.

Then, having done what Harley had told him to do, and having done it well and thoroughly, he went back to the hotel — his own hotel, not the one where he had dumped the paper and the bills — and went to sleep.

In the morning he read in the newspapers that Harley had been killed, and he was stunned. It didn't seem possible. He couldn't believe it; it was a joke someone was playing on him. Harley would come back to him, he knew. And he was right; Harley did, but that was later, in the swamp.

But anyway, Justin had to know, so he took the very next train for Albany. He must have been on the train when the police went to his hotel, and at the hotel they must have learned he'd asked at the desk about trains for Albany, because they were waiting for him when he got off the train there.

They took him to a station and they kept him there a long long time, days and days, asking him questions. They found out, after a while, that he couldn't have killed Harley because he'd been in New York City at the time Harley was killed in Albany, but they knew also that he and Harley had been operating the little mint, and they thought that might be a lead to who killed Harley, and they were interested in the counterfeiting, too, maybe even more than in the murder. They asked Justin Dean questions, over and over and over, and he couldn't answer them, so he didn't. They kept him awake for days at a time, asking him questions over and over. Most of all they wanted to know where the plates were. He wished he could tell them that the plates were safe where nobody could ever get them again, but he couldn't tell them that without admitting that he and Harley had been counterfeiting, so he couldn't tell them.

They located the Amsterdam shop, but they didn't find any evidence there, and they really had no evidence to hold Justin on at all, but he didn't know that, and it never occurred to him to get a lawyer.

He kept wanting to see Harley, and they wouldn't let him; then, when they learned he really didn't believe Harley could be dead, they made him look at a dead man they said was Harley, and he guessed it was, although Harley looked different dead. He didn't look magnificent, dead. And Justin believed, then, but still didn't believe. And after that he just went silent and wouldn't say a word, even when they kept him awake for days and days with a bright light in his eyes, and kept slapping him to keep him awake. They didn't use clubs or rubber hoses, but they slapped him a million times and wouldn't let him sleep. And after a while he lost track of things and couldn't have answered their questions even if he'd wanted to.

For a while after that, he was in a bed in a white room, and all he remembers about that are nightmares he had, and calling for Harley and an awful confusion as to whether Harley was dead or not; and then things came back to him gradually and he knew he didn't want to stay in the white room; he wanted to get out so he could hunt for Harley. And if Harley was dead, he wanted to kill whoever had killed Harley, because Harley would have done the same for him.

So he began pretending, and acting, very cleverly, the way the doctors and nurses seemed to want him to act, and after a while they gave him his clothes and let him go.

He was becoming cleverer now. He thought, *What would Harley tell me to do?* And he knew they'd try to follow him because they'd think he might lead them to the plates, which they didn't know were at the bottom of the bay, and he gave them the slip before he left Albany, and he went first to Boston, and from there by boat to New York, instead of going direct.

He went first to the print shop, and went in the back way after watching the alley for a long time to be sure the place wasn't guarded. It was a mess; they must have searched it very thoroughly for the plates.

Harley wasn't there, of course. Justin left and from a phone booth in a drugstore he telephoned their hotel and asked for Harley and was told Harley no longer lived there; and to be clever and not let them guess who he was, he asked for Justin Dean, and they said Justin Dean didn't live there any more either.

Then he moved to a different drugstore, and from there he decided to call up some friends of Harley's, and he phoned Bull Mallon first, and because Bull was a friend, he told him who he was and asked if he knew where Harley was.

Bull Mallon didn't pay any attention to that; he sounded excited, a little, and he asked, "Did the cops get the plates, Dean?" and Justin said they didn't, that he wouldn't tell them, and he asked again about Harley.

Bull asked, "Are you nuts, or kidding?" And Justin just asked him again, and Bull's voice changed and he said, "Where are you?" and Justin told him. Bull said, "Harley's here. He's staying under cover, but it's all right if you know, Dean. You wait right there at the drugstore, and we'll come and get you."

They came and got Justin, Bull Mallon and two other men in a car; and they told him Harley was hiding out way deep in New Jersey and that they were going to drive there now. So he went along and sat in the back seat between two men he didn't know, while Bull Mallon drove.

It was late afternoon then, when they picked him up, and Bull drove all evening and most of the night and he drove fast, so he must have gone farther than New Jersey, at least into Virginia or maybe farther, into the Carolinas. The sky was getting faintly gray with first dawn when they stopped at a rustic cabin that looked like it had been used as a hunting lodge. It was miles from anywhere, there wasn't even a road leading to it, just a trail that was level enough for the car to be able to make it.

They took Justin into the cabin and tied him to a chair,

and they told him Harley wasn't there, but Harley had told them that Justin would tell them where the plates were, and he couldn't leave until he did tell.

Justin didn't believe them; he knew then that they'd tricked him about Harley, but it didn't matter, as far as the plates were concerned. It didn't matter if he told them what he'd done with the plates, because they couldn't get them again, and they wouldn't tell the police. So he told them, quite willingly.

But they didn't believe him. They said he'd hidden the plates and was lying. They tortured him to make him tell. They beat him, and they cut him with knives, and they held burning matches and lighted cigars to the soles of his feet, and they pushed needles under his fingernails. Then they'd rest and ask him questions and if he could talk, he'd tell them the truth, and after a while they'd start to torture him again.

It went on for days and weeks — Justin doesn't know how long, but it was a long time. Once they went away for several days and left him tied up with nothing to eat or drink. They came back and started in all over again. And all the time he hoped Harley would come to help him, but Harley didn't come, not then.

After a while what was happening in the cabin ended, or anyway he didn't know any more about it. They must have thought he was dead; maybe they were right, or anyway not far from wrong.

The next thing he knows was the swamp. He was lying in shallow water at the edge of deeper water. His face was out of the water; it woke him when he turned a little and his face went under. They must have thought him dead and thrown him into the water, but he had floated into the shallow part before he had drowned, and a last flicker of consciousness had turned him over on his back with his face out.

I don't remember much about Justin in the swamp; it was a long time, but I just remember flashes of it. I couldn't move at first; I just lay there in the shallow water with my face out. It got dark and it got cold, I remember, and finally my arms would move a little and I got farther out of the water, lying in the mud with only my feet in the water. I slept or was unconscious again and when I woke up it was getting gray dawn, and that was when Harley came. I think I'd been calling him, and he must have heard.

He stood there, dressed as immaculately and perfectly as ever, right in the swamp; and he was laughing at me for being so weak and lying there like a log, half in the dirty water and half in the mud, and I got up and nothing hurt any more.

We shook hands and he said, "Come on, Justin, let's get you out of here," and I was so glad he'd come that I cried a little. He laughed at me for that and said I should lean on him and he'd help me walk, but I wouldn't do that, because I was coated with mud and filth of the swamp and he was so clean and perfect in a white linen suit, like an ad in a magazine. And all the way out of that swamp, all the days and nights we spent there, he never even got mud on his trouser cuffs, nor his hair mussed.

I told him just to lead the way; and he did, walking just ahead of me, sometimes turning around, laughing and talking to me and cheering me up. Sometimes I'd fall but I wouldn't let him come back and help me. But he'd wait patiently until I could get up. Sometimes I'd crawl instead when I couldn't stand up any more. Sometimes I'd have to swim streams that he'd leap lightly across.

And it was day and night and day and night, and sometimes I'd sleep, and things would crawl across me. And some of them I caught and ate, or maybe I dreamed that. I remember other things, in that swamp, like an organ that played a lot of the time, and sometimes angels in the air and devils in the water, but those were delirium, I guess.

Harley would say, "A little farther, Justin; we'll make it. And we'll get back at them, at all of them."

And we made it. We came to dry fields, cultivated fields with waist-high corn, but there weren't ears on the corn for me to eat. And then there was a stream, a clear stream that wasn't stinking water like the swamp, and Harley told me to wash myself and my clothes and I did, although I wanted to hurry on to where I could get food.

I still looked pretty bad; my clothes were clean of mud and filth but they were mere rags and wet, because I couldn't wait for them to dry, and I had a ragged beard and I was barefoot.

But we went on and came to a little farm building, just a two-room shack, and there was a smell of fresh bread just out of an oven, and I ran the last few yards to knock on the door. A woman, an ugly woman, opened the door and when she saw me she slammed it again before I could say a word.

Strength came to me from somewhere, maybe from Harley, although I can't remember him being there just then. There was a pile of kindling logs beside the door. I picked one of them up as though it were no heavier than a broomstick, and I broke down the door and killed the woman. She screamed a lot, but I killed her. Then I ate the hot fresh bread.

I watched from the window as I ate, and saw a man running across the field toward the house. I found a knife, and I killed him as he came in at the door. It was much better, killing with the knife; I liked it that way.

I ate more bread, and kept watching from all the windows, but no one else came. Then my stomach hurt from the hot bread I'd eaten; and I had to lie down, doubled up; and when the hurting quit, I slept.

Harley woke me up, and it was dark. He said, "Let's get going; you should be far away from here before it's daylight."

I knew he was right, but I didn't hurry away. I was becoming, as you see, very clever now. I knew there were things to do first. I found matches and a lamp, and lighted the lamp. Then I hunted through the shack for everything I could use. I found clothes of the man, and they fitted me — not too badly except that I had to turn up the cuffs of the trousers and the shirt. His shoes were big, but that was good because my feet were so swollen.

I found a razor and shaved; it took a long time because my

hand wasn't steady, but I was very careful and didn't cut myself much.

I had to hunt hardest for their money, but I found it finally. It was sixty dollars.

And I took the knife, after I had sharpened it. It isn't fancy; just a bone-handled carving knife, but it's good steel. I'll show it to you, pretty soon now. It's had a lot of use.

Then we left and it was Harley who told me to stay away from the roads and find railroad tracks. That was easy because we heard a train whistle far off in the night and knew which direction the tracks lay. From then on, with Harley helping, it's been easy.

You won't need the details from here. I mean, about the brakeman, and about the tramp we found asleep in the empty reefer, and about the near thing I had with the police in Richmond. I learned from that; I learned I mustn't talk to Harley when anybody else was around to hear. He hides himself from them; he's got a trick and they don't know he's there, and they think I'm funny in the head if I talk to him. But in Richmond I bought better clothes and got a haircut, and a man I killed in an alley had forty dollars on him, so I had money again. I've done a lot of traveling since then. If you stop to think you'll know where I am right now.

I'm looking for Bull Mallon and the two men who helped him. Their names are Harry and Carl. I'm going to kill them when I find them. Harley keeps telling me that those fellows are big time and that I'm not ready for them yet. But I can be looking while I'm getting ready so I keep moving around. Sometimes I stay in one place long enough to hold a job as a printer for a while. I've learned a lot of things. I can hold a job and people don't think I'm too strange; they don't get scared when I look at them like they sometimes did a few months ago. And I've learned not to talk to Harley except in our own room and then only very quietly so people in the next room won't think I'm talking to myself.

And I've kept in practice with the knife. I've killed lots of people with it, mostly on the streets at night. Sometimes because they look like they might have money on them, but mostly just for practice and because I've come to like doing it. I'm really good with the knife by now. You'll hardly feel it.

But Harley tells me that kind of killing is easy and that it's something else to kill a person who's on guard, as Bull and Harry and Carl will be.

And that's the conversation that led to the bet I mentioned. I told Harley that I'd bet him that, right now, I could warn a man I was going to use the knife on him and even tell him why and approximately when, and that I could still kill him. And he bet me that I couldn't, and he's going to lose that bet.

He's going to lose it because I'm warning you right now and you're not going to believe me. I'm betting that you're going to believe that this is just another story in a book. That you won't believe that this is the *only* copy of this book that contains this story and that this story is true. Even when I tell you how it was done, I don't think you'll really believe me.

You see I'm putting it over on Harley, winning the bet, by putting it over on you. He never thought, and you won't realize how easy it is for a good printer, who's been a counterfeiter too, to counterfeit one story in a book. Nothing like as hard as counterfeiting a five dollar bill.

I had to pick a book of short stories and I picked this one because I happened to notice that the last story in the book was titled *Don't Look Behind You* and that was going to be a good title for this. You'll see what I mean in a few minutes.

I'm lucky that the printing shop I'm working for now does book work and had a type face that matches the rest of this book. I had a little trouble matching the paper exactly, but I finally did and I've got it ready while I'm writing this. I'm writing this directly on a Linotype, late at night in the shop where I'm working days. I even have the boss's permission, told him I was going to set up and print a story that a friend of mine had written, as a surprise for him, and that I'd melt the type metal back as soon as I'd printed one good copy.

When I finish writing this I'll make up the type in pages to match the rest of the book and I'll print it on the matching paper I have ready. I'll cut the new pages to fit and bind them in; you won't be able to tell the difference, even if a faint suspicion may cause you to look at it. Don't forget I made five and ten dollar bills you couldn't have told from the original, and this is kindergarten stuff compared to that job. And I've done enough bookbinding that I'll be able to take the last story out of the book and bind this one in instead of it and you won't be able to tell the difference no matter how closely you look. I'm going to do a perfect job of it if it takes me all night.

And tomorrow I'll go to some bookstore, or maybe a newsstand or even a drugstore that sells books and has other copies of this book, ordinary copies, and I'll plant this one there. I'll find myself a good place to watch from, and I'll be watching when you buy it.

The rest I can't tell you yet because it depends a lot on circumstances, whether you went right home with the book or what you did. I won't know till I follow you and keep watch till you read it-and I see that you're reading the last story in the book.

If you're home while you're reading this, maybe I'm in the house with you right now. Maybe I'm in this very room, hidden, waiting for you to finish the story. Maybe I'm watching through a window. Or maybe I'm sitting near you on the streetcar or train, if you're reading it there. Maybe I'm on the fire escape outside your hotel room. But wherever you're reading it, I'm near you, watching and waiting for you to finish. You can count on that.

You're pretty near the end now. You'll be finished in seconds and you'll close the book, still not believing. Or, if you haven't read the stories in order, maybe you'll turn back to start another story. If you do, you'll never finish it.

But don't look around; you'll be happier if you don't know, if you don't see the knife coming. When I kill people from behind they don't seem to mind so much.

Go on, just a few seconds or minutes, thinking this is just another story. Don't look behind you. Don't believe this — *until you feel the knife.*

THE END

www.ingramcontent.com/pod-product-compliance
Lightning Source LLC
Chambersburg PA
CBHW020149180626
46810CB00004B/1801